THE
TREASURE

A Clint Smith Thriller

Bob Doerr

TotalRecall Publications, Inc.
1103 Middlecreek
Friendswood, Texas 77546
281-992-3131
www.mousegate.com

Copyright © 2021 by: Bob Doerr
All rights reserved
ISBN: 978-1-64883-084-6
UPC: 6-43977-40846-4
Library of Congress Control Number: 2021935878

Printed in the United States of America with simultaneous printings in Australia, Canada, and United Kingdom.

FIRST EDITION
1 2 3 4 5 6 7 8 9 10

This is a work of fiction. The characters, names, events, views, and subject matter of this book are either the author's imagination or are used fictitiously. Any similarity or resemblance to any real people, real situations or actual events is purely coincidental and not intended to portray any person, place, or event in a false, disparaging or negative light.

TO THOSE WHO SERVE.

I thank all the first responders and
care givers who sacrifice their time
and safety for the rest of us.

Award Winning Author: Bob Doerr

grew up in a military family, graduated from the Air Force Academy, and had a career of his own in the Air Force. Bob specialized in criminal investigations and counter-intelligence gaining significant insight to the worlds of crime, espionage, and terrorism. His work brought him into close coordination with the security agencies of many countries and filled his mind with the fascinating plots and characters found in his books today. His education credits include a Masters in International Relations from Creighton University. A full-time author with eighteen published books and a co-author in another, Bob was selected by the Military Writers Society of America as its Author of the Year for 2013. The Eric Hoffer Awards awarded No One Else to Kill its 2013 first runner up to the grand prize for commercial fiction. His other books have also garnered a number of medals and recognition. Bob lives in Garden Ridge, Texas, with Leigh, his wife of 48 years, and Cinco, their ornery cat.

About the Book

The Treasure is the fourth book in the Clint Smith thriller series. After a successful mission in South America, Clint heads to Las Vegas on vacation and to dig up a stagecoach strong box he had found in the desert earlier but had not opened. Upon inspection, he finds some old gold coins in mint condition and some well-preserved documents. He gives the contents of the strong box to a lawyer to find buyers. One of the documents, unfortunately, creates a maelstrom of violence and murder, and puts Clint squarely in the cross hairs of some Chinese assassins. Clint leaves Las Vegas to keep out of the spotlight, only to find himself going to Alaska in an attempt to rescue a female police officer who had been assigned to protect him in Las Vegas.

CHAPTER 1

The spider had to be five inches across, large even by South American standards. Clint figured it belonged to the tarantula family, and it crawled across the leaves and twigs in front of Clint's face. He liked to tell people that snakes and spiders didn't scare him, but the mere eight inches of separation had him questioning that bravado.

The real problem, Clint told himself, wasn't the spider, but the fact that he couldn't move away from the spider without alerting the four, heavily armed men standing barely forty feet away. When Clint chose this spot in the thick undergrowth in which to crawl to and hide, he never expected anyone to get this close to him. Maybe the spider was an omen.

He had been hunting for Miguel Opisbo Ferma in the jungles of the Amazon for the past three days. His pursuit had taken him through two other South American countries and had finally led him here. The large, manicured yard started about five feet in front of him and covered about an acre of land cleared out of the surrounding jungle. In the middle of the yard sat a modern looking, single story house. He guessed there wasn't another house for miles around.

Clint could see Ferma's black Cadillac SUV parked in the circular driveway along with a blue Toyota sedan. He hadn't seen Ferma, but Buzz had reassured him that Ferma was here. Attempts to get the Brazilian government to take any kind of action against Ferma had been ignored. One could hardly blame them, since he had done nothing wrong in Brazil. So, while the rest of the U.S. intelligence community debated what to do, Clint's boss, Theresa Deer, sent him after Ferma.

Of course, Deer and her small office had a distinct advantage over the rest of huge American intelligence apparatus. No one, well almost no one, knew that her office even existed. Besides, no one would care if Ferma suddenly disappeared.

For the last decade, Ferma had left a trail of dead bodies throughout Central America. He allegedly had his hands in kidnappings, human smuggling, and drug trafficking. Not so much that he ran these operations, but he had become the enforcer or muscle behind a lot of the organized criminal operations in the countries north of Brazil and south of Mexico. He had a lot of blood on his hands. Worse yet from the American leadership point of view, Ferma had begun using his clout to intimidate the political leadership in the region.

The four men had been pacing around the yard, and boredom had brought them together to gossip, complain, and smoke. In some weird coincidence and to Clint's misfortune, they had chosen to stop a few yards away from Clint. Thankfully, the security team didn't have any guard dogs. Clint lay still, and the spider moved on.

On his part, Clint had not come up with a way to get into the house, but that didn't matter. Opportunity would show its face, and Clint would have to be ready for it.

Sometimes, however, opportunity comes in strange and unexpected ways. On this day, it came in the form of a large spider that left Clint and began crawling toward the four, armed men. It moved out of the thick underbrush and onto the well-manicured yard. The movement quickly caught the eyes of one of the men who informed the others. All four men approached the spider, bringing them closer to Clint.

The inevitable happened. The men looked back along the trail of the spider to see if there might be a second spider, and one of the men spotted Clint. The man shouted and started to raise his weapon.

Clint moved faster. He fired twice, and the two shots hit the first man in his chest. The other three guards responded to their colleague's shout by raising their weapons, but they had not seen Clint. The two rounds fired by Clint gave them his location; however, the shots had more of an effect to frighten them, and all three jerked sideways or backwards. Two of the men made the mistake of staring at their fellow guard collapsing to the ground.

Clint shot each of the men and then shot them again as they were falling. Two rounds always worked better than one. Shouts came from the house, and two armed men rushed out. Rather than approach the area around the fallen men, the two men shot wildly in Clint's direction. He saw a man whom he believed to be Ferma race out of the house to the Cadillac. A second man ran beside him.

Scooting backwards before turning around, Clint crawled for about twenty yards before he started sprinting to the spot where he had hidden his motorcycle. While he may not have had a Plan A, he did have a Plan B, which he hoped would now work. He drove the motorcycle down a rough, dirt road that had likely been cut out to give the original construction workers access to the lot now occupied by Ferma's house.

This mostly overgrown road intersected with the newer, paved road that led to the house. The new road curved to the left, if one was driving away from the house, a few yards past the intersection of the new road with the old. Clint had pulled a large piece of a fallen tree onto the road at the end of that curve, hoping to stop Ferma's vehicle and thereby expose him for a moment. This was his Plan B.

Clint watched Ferma's Cadillac race by seconds before he reached the paved road. He followed it around the curve in time to see it swerve to miss the tree in the road. The driver lost control of the vehicle, and it veered off the road, slamming into a live tree. Clint stopped behind the vehicle, got off the motorcycle, and moved up along the driver's side. He had his Beretta 9mm pistol in hand. The driver already had his own pistol in his hand and was attempting to get out of the car. He moved clumsily and appeared stunned but started to aim his pistol at Clint. Clint shot him in his chest and then shot over the slumped body of the driver, hitting Ferma in the head. He climbed back onto his motorcycle and drove off.

CHAPTER 2

Clint ran along the beach and watched the storm clouds grow in the sky. He noticed some new construction north of the city and thought that one of these days even more people will discover the beauty of South Padre Island. When they did, he figured he would have to run a few more miles to reach the quiet, remoteness he could now reach just ten minutes from his condo. His phone buzzed, and he slowed down to a walk.

"Hello," he said. He didn't have to identify himself, as no one but his bosses in D.C. had this number. If a phone other than the few programmed into his phone tried to call him, the call went immediately into voice mail. This month the voice mail would identify the phone as belonging to Empire Construction. The phone contained the newest security technology available to the U.S. government.

"Welcome back," Theresa Deer said. She knew Clint had been back for over a week, but this was the first time she had spoken to him since he had returned.

"Thank you, and how are you doing? Fully recovered?"

"Yes, but for some reason the CIA is being very nosy about what happened to Ferma."

"I wouldn't think they would care."

"Neither did I, and that's what has me concerned," Deer said. "They've been doing some checks on me and the office ever since I returned from Korea. They hate not knowing things."

"How do I fit into all this?"

"I want you to take some time off. Go somewhere, but drive and make it hard for someone to trace you. You deserve a month off."

"Think they can find me here?" I asked.

"It's possible, not likely but possible. I know they're trying, and that's my concern. They have a team looking into Ferma's death, and I don't believe they give a damn that he's dead. They just want to know who did it, and why they were out of the loop. Fortunately, things are quiet here for the moment, so I have all the hunters keeping a low profile."

"I can be on the road this afternoon."

"Good, and listen," Deer said, "relax and have a good time. I mean it. You deserve it."

As the call ended, Clint turned around and jogged back to his condo. He had plenty of places he could go and disappear, but Las Vegas held the top spot. He had intended to go there after returning from Korea, but the Ferma op preempted his trip.

Being single, having no pets and no obligations made leaving on a short notice easy. He always had a travel bag ready for a quick departure, something he had first learned in the military. Besides, where he would be going, he could easily purchase anything he needed later.

At four in the afternoon, Clint crossed over the causeway that joined the island to the mainland, Texas, and started his journey west. His new, black Lincoln MKZ had a full tank of gas, and a Yeti mug topped off with hot coffee sat in the cup holder next to him. He would grab something to eat when he stopped for gas or a bathroom break. Unless traffic slowed him, which was a probability traveling through San Antonio, he could reach Kerrville before eleven.

Kerrville, Texas, is like so many small cities that have an interstate highway running through them. A number of chain hotels and restaurants lined the few exits, allowing travelers to take a break from their journeys, and Clint knew all of the hotels and restaurants would prefer to be paid in cash, no questions asked.

Driving gave Clint time to think. While he didn't mind being told to disappear for a while, in fact, he looked forward to his vacation, he couldn't help but think that there had to be a better way to run a country. Well, he thought, maybe running a country was giving his job a little more importance than it merited.

"Who we are and what we do have to be kept secret," Buzz had explained to him. He had already had a similar briefing by Deer when he joined her small team. Buzz, her deputy, had wanted to add his two cents. "We were created after nine eleven to serve a very small and precise mission. The President needed something that would allow him to cut through the quagmire of bureaucracy, in fighting, and political backstabbing. The country needed something that could give special, and that's the key word, special threats a laser like focus and quick results. We're not a rogue agency, but I sometimes think many parts of the government might label us as one if our existence ever came to light."

"But why would that be?" Clint had asked.

"While our creation resulted from top secret discussions among a small handful of our nation's top leaders, other than the initial memo, there has been no paper trail, no audits, and no real oversight. That's the way it was designed. The only way we could remain a secret. My guess is that our current president may not even know we exist. Of course, he may, but with all the classified projects out there, he literally has no time to be briefed on all of them."

"So, who tells us what to do?" Clint asked.

"Here's where we get to our real strength and, if compromised, perhaps our greatest weakness. Deer makes the call. She has a boss, if you can call him that, near the top of the National Security Council, but they rarely contact each other. Again, secrecy is the utmost important thing."

"So, the CIA, NSA, DoD and the rest don't know of our existence?"

"Correct," Buzz said with a smile. "Our government has had agencies do what we do forever. The CIA and DoD still do them, but they are subject to discovery, compromise, and all types of political fallout and criticism. We are not here to replace them, but to provide a quiet, surgical strike where needed, and with no trail left behind."

"You know, we don't even have an official name. We call ourselves Special Section or Section, but you won't find that in writing anywhere. We're identified in the Intelligence budget by some acronym and a description that is itself classified but has nothing to do with our real mission. The plaque on the door implies we do multi-disciplinary threat analyses for the US Marshall Service. That we do, and we do it quite well, but that's just to keep everyone happy. The leadership in the Marshall Service know we don't work for them, but even they have been given a cover story. We don't affect their budget, they get our intelligence reports, so everyone is happy."

Over the years, Clint had come to realize the value of the

small team of hunters to which he belonged. He also wondered, since a few months ago they had been instrumental in keeping the president from being assassinated, if someone may have briefed the president at the time on the existence of Section.

"We are unique, in one other way," Buzz added. "In a government of bloated bureaucracy and waste, we are tiny. Hidden within the U.S. Marshall Service, our budget is smaller than most acceptable rounding errors of the other government agencies. We have less than twenty people on the entire budget."

The numbers surprised him, but Clint had since learned that being small hadn't hurt the team's effectiveness. Though he never understood the technical process, he knew that Section had access to almost everything that was logged into any network throughout the U.S. Intelligence Community. They also had massive, dedicated computing power to stay on top of all that data.

As expected, Clint had no trouble finding a hotel in Kerrville. Next door to the hotel, he treated himself to a late night, enchilada dinner. It took him another two days to reach Las Vegas, where he checked into the Orleans Hotel. Clint had stayed there a couple years earlier and liked the fact that it was off the strip. He doubted anyone at the hotel would remember him, not that it really mattered. The only person who might was a woman whom he had helped with a boyfriend problem. The guy considered himself a big-time gangster and felt like she was his property. He was no longer a problem.

CHAPTER 3

Clint leaned against his car, hot and frustrated. The last time he visited Las Vegas, he had found himself on top of this hill waiting and watching for an ambush of a Greek billionaire. While waiting and in an effort to not look too conspicuous, he had walked around with a metal detector slightly above the ground. At the time, he wasn't actually looking for anything and thought the effort was kind of corny. Then as today, he could see for miles in all directions from this vantage point, but other than the light traffic below, he couldn't see a single person. Not that anyone had any interest in some fool looking for something out here.

Yet, he did discover something back then. He wasn't trying to, but he did. He discovered what had appeared to be an old, small strong box, something that a stage coach may have carried to protect valuables. He used a metal detector and found it barely an inch underground; however, just as he was scraping the dirt off the top of it, his surveillance turned operational, and he had to leave. He barely had time to cover the strong box with loose dirt.

Clint walked over to the edge of the hill and looked down at the highway. Give or take ten yards, this had to be the spot. He tried to remember the exact location where he had parked, and where he had located the strong box. The terrain consisted of dirt, sand, rocks of all sizes and a variety of grasses and weeds sparsely spread out on the ground. He went back to the car and drank some water out of a plastic Dasani bottle.

For the second time, he checked the charge on the metal detector and made sure the bottom of the detector was clean. Everything appeared in working order. He decided to go at his search in a different manner. Rather than walk in ever larger circles in one general area, Clint decided to walk in a straight line on the south side of the dirt road for about twenty yards, sweeping the detector back and forth to cover about a yard in each sweep. He would then return along a straight line a little further away from the road.

Clint had selected Las Vegas as his initial destination, because he wanted to see what was in the box. It might be empty, but its existence had been on his mind for a while, and he wanted some resolution.

He had taken twenty steps and decided to take a couple more before turning around. Just as he was starting to turn, the metal detector swept over something that caused the instrument to start chirping.

"Eureka!" Clint said and leaned close to the ground that hid the object. He didn't see any sign that the ground had ever been disturbed, not even any evidence that he had been here a couple years earlier. Of course, with the rain, wind, and the hot desert sun, the ground could have resettled.

He left the detector to insure he wouldn't lose the spot again and retrieved the hand spade and shovel from his car. A few minutes later, Clint had unearthed the strong box. The box measured eighteen inches in length, ten inches wide, and eight inches tall. Long ago, someone had broken the metal clasp that would normally keep it shut. Clint didn't see a lock or the missing pieces of the clasp in the hole he had dug and imagined the damage was done elsewhere before the box was buried.

Faded remains of something painted on the top of the box had lost so much of their coloring and definition that Clint could only read the letters e and s.

Clint carried everything back to his car and put the detector and the tools in his trunk before opening the box. A leather bag, still in good shape, further insulated the items in the box. He removed the leather bag and began sorting out its contents, placing one item at a time onto the hood of his car. He used a rock to keep the pages from being blown away by the dust flavored breeze. Most of the contents consisted of documents, with individual, multi-page documents separated by a thin cord or ribbon. Single page documents were bunched together. Clint thought a museum or history buff might consider this a big find, but nothing looked too interesting to him.

He also pulled out a small leather pouch tied shut. The weight and jingling sound that came from the pouch when Clint rattled it intrigued him, so he wasn't surprised when he poured out seventeen gold coins onto the stack of documents. Both the bag and the box had the capacity to hold more pouches of the same size, and Clint wondered if originally there had been more. Years ago, if there had been, the person who had buried the strong box may have taken the other pouches of coins and had planned to return to retrieve this last bag. For any of a variety of reasons, he had been unable to do so.

Clint didn't have a lot of knowledge about gold or old gold coins, but he didn't need much to realize these had to be valuable. They looked to be in mint condition. He put all the items back in the leather bag, and then back in the strong box, before putting the box in the trunk of his car.

Driving back to the hotel, Clint considered how to best handle his discovery. He didn't need any money the coins could bring him, although he thought he would like to keep one coin as a souvenir. However, the history or mystery behind the box and its contents piqued his interest.

At the hotel, he sat in his room and scoured the internet for a local museum or historical society that had the expertise and interest in reviewing what he had found. He glanced at a couple that seemed promising and noticed they both had the same lawyer on their Board of Directors. That gave him an idea.

He called the number for William B. Forthsyte, Esq., and the call was answered on the first ring.

"Mr. Forthsyte's offices, Melanie speaking. How may I assist you?" Melanie had an Australian accent and had the line well-rehearsed.

They kept the conversation short, and thanks to a previous appointment falling through, Melanie offered and Clint accepted an afternoon appointment for the next day. She never asked him why he wanted to see Forthsyte.

Clint spent the rest of the day poolside and the evening in the casino slowly losing thirty dollars at the roulette table.

CHAPTER 4

"This is amazing," Forthsyte said, going through the documents from the strong box. "I doubt if you can appreciate the value these would be to a museum or even to the university. I don't mean money-wise, I'm sorry to say. They might pay you something for them but not much."

"I'm not here trying to get rich," Clint said. "I find them intriguing, too, and would like to know what, if any, historical significance they might have."

Forthsyte looked at him skeptically. "Of course, the coins are valuable."

"Of course, but they're not going to set me for life or even for a decade."

Forthsyte glanced back at the documents and thumbed through them again, stopping and reading a couple in detail. "Most of these are no more than what would be sent by email today. Their real value is the fact that they are over a hundred years old and appear to be genuine. Two of these documents are land deeds. With all the death and mayhem throughout the early years of this region over land ownership, these could become interesting, but again, not worth much."

Clint nodded and took a sip of coffee. The lawyer was a tall, very thin man, who reminded him of an elementary school teacher he once had. Clint and his friends had called the teacher Skeletor in reference to the comic book villain who was a human skeleton. According to a diploma on the wall, Forthsyte had graduated from law school over twenty years earlier.

"What would you like me to do with all this?" Forthsyte asked.

"A couple of things. First, I'd rather my name be kept out of all this."

"Not a problem. This is Las Vegas, we're very good at keeping names out of things."

"I'd like you to give the documents to the best places for them, but I would like a written summary of what each document is, along with any background that would not be that hard for you to discover."

Forthsyte nodded. "I recommend you charge a small stipend, making the transfer official with a bill of sale. I can sign it for you and negotiate everything."

"Good. Finally, can the coins be sold to a collector or someone, or do they need to be turned over to the government?"

"Good lord, Mr. Smith, we don't turn things over to the government. We spend a great deal of time trying to limit what they take from us."

Clint smiled. "I'd like to keep one of the coins and take it with me."

"Absolutely, they are yours."

"I'd like a receipt for the sale of the coins, but if you would like to keep one as part of your fee that is fine with me."

"Thank you, this has been a fascinating visit. If you are free this Friday, I believe I can have everything accomplished and ready for you by then. I'll need you to call Melanie first thing Friday morning. She can give you the particulars for everything, and you can give us the okay to close all the arrangements. Friday afternoon we can meet, and I can give you the receipts, summaries, and a check with your proceeds. Would that be satisfactory?"

"Sounds marvelous."

"And you said you would like to keep your identity confidential."

"At least for the time being."

"I understand," Forthsyte said, stood and extended his hand and Clint did the same. Outside in the receptionist office, Melanie stood waiting for Clint. He wondered if she had listened in on the whole conversation, or if Forthsyte had given her some signal.

"Here is our card, Mr. Smith. I'll be waiting for your call."

Clint guessed he stood at least a foot taller than Melanie. Her very short blond hair made her blue eyes the natural focal point on her face, and not a bad focal point at that.

"Is that accent Australian?" he asked.

"Yes, it came with me when I came here. I attended UNLV, and much to my parents' chagrin, I decided to stay after graduation."

"I've never been to Australia."

"You should go sometime."

"I would need a tour guide," Clint said.

"Oh, there are lots of them over there." She smiled, "Friday, then?"

"I'll call you Friday morning," Clint said, returning the smile and leaving the office.

In the parking lot, Clint fingered the solitary gold coin in his pocket and wondered if Forthsyte would be able to get everything done by Friday. He didn't linger on the question long, realizing Forthsyte already knew all the right contacts.

Forthsyte could probably have the deal done by phone tonight and spend all day tomorrow, Thursday, figuring out how much he could rip off Clint.

His phone buzzed in his pocket.

"Hello," he said into the phone.

"Hey, Clint, how is everything going?" Buzz asked.

"Good. What's up?"

"Not much here. Just a reminder that we need you to keep a low profile, and we're hoping you didn't return to Las Vegas to finish some unfinished business."

"Actually, I am taking care of some unfinished business, but it doesn't involve any other people. I should be out of here by the weekend and not see or speak to anyone whom I had contact with before."

"Great. Sorry to be nosy, but Deer is a little paranoid right now, and everything everywhere is on hold," Buzz said.

"Well, if it's that slow, you should take a short vacation yourself."

"Wish I could, but we've been busy pumping out regional threat analyses."

"Oh, lucky you."

"Actually, it's one thing I'm good at, and it helps with our cover."

"I'm thinking of going to Canada next, to Lake Babine in British Columbia. Great fishing there, and I haven't done any in a while. You should join me for a couple of days," Clint said.

"Wish I could, but there's no way I could get away now. Send me some pictures though."

"Okay."

"Besides, I hear there are a lot of female anglers in Canada.

You can probably find one to keep you better company than I would be for you."

"I'll keep that in mind."

"Well, have a nice vacation, and sorry to be checking up on you."

"That's okay. Talk to you later." Clint drove away from Forthsyte's office and stopped at the new Las Vegas Raiders football stadium. The stadium would be open soon for its first professional game. Unfortunately, the city or the new owners had the stadium locked up tight. Clint decided the walk around it was sufficient exercise for one day and returned to his hotel. The poolside and the warm sun beckoned him.

CHAPTER 5

Thursday didn't bring any surprises or excitement. He continued his losing streak in the casino, but he gambled with so little money he didn't mind. Besides, he thought, the sale of the gold coins would more than cover the cost of his entire vacation.

Early Friday morning, he called Melanie.

"Mr. Forthsyte's offices, Melanie speaking, how may I assist you?"

"Hi, Melanie, this is Clint Smith."

"Yes, good to hear from you. I'm very happy to let you know that Mr. Forthsyte has finished everything. Would you like to write this down, or do you have a good memory?"

"My memory is pretty good, go ahead."

"He has secured a buyer for all the documents except for the property deeds for one thousand dollars. He said you knew not to expect much from them."

"That's right. The amount is fine, but more important is a summary of what each document is or contains."

"Yes, Mr. Forthsyte has already done that."

"Great."

"You'll be glad to know he has found a buyer for the coins. He said to tell you the purchase price is very good, and that he will accept one coin as the payment for his services. You'll receive fifty-one thousand dollars for the coins? Does that meet your expectations?"

"I didn't have any expectations, so yes the amount is fine

with me. What will he be doing with the land deeds?"

"He still has those here in the office, although I believe he made copies and is out researching them this morning."

"That's fine. When should I come by?"

"His note says that he would like for you to come at two this afternoon. Would that work for you?"

"That would be perfect." He thought about asking Melanie out for lunch to celebrate the sale, but let the phone call end before doing so.

He arrived at Forthsyte's office at exactly two and caught Melanie sitting in one of the large comfortable chairs reading a paperback. She jumped up when Clint walked in.

"Oh, I let the time sneak up on me," she said. She moved behind her desk and stood next to her chair.

"Good book?" Clint asked.

"Oh, this? One of those historical stories. It's quite good." She put the book down on her desk. "I don't know where Mr. Forthsyte is, but it's not like him to miss an appointment. You're welcome to wait here, or next door there's a coffee shop. I'm sure he'll be here any minute."

"Have you talked to him?"

"Three times this morning," she shrugged her shoulders.

Clint looked around the office. "Anything to read?"

Melanie looked at Clint for a second like she was trying to think of something. She smiled and held up the book she was reading.

Clint read the title Roses on the book's cover.

"Oh, wait a second," she said, turning and grabbing a folder off the top of the safe behind her. "I guess you can have this. After all, it is yours. I'll need you to sign the receipt. That way you would have read everything by the time Mr. Forthsyte gets back and can discuss everything with him."

"Can I take it down to the coffee shop with me?"

"Yes, of course." Melanie opened the folder and separated the contents into three stacks on her desk. "These are copies of the documents along with descriptions and background on each. Here are the two checks, and these last two items are the receipts. One for the coins and one for the documents. After you sign the receipts, I'll make you copies of each, too."

"Looks official enough for me," Clint said and started to read the lengthy paragraph below the signature block on the receipt.

"That's just the standard legal mumbo-jumbo," Melanie said.

"Do I need to hire another lawyer to explain to me what it says?" Clint asked, smiling.

"No, not at all."

"Just kidding," Clint said. He signed the two receipts, and Melanie promptly made copies for him. She put everything back in the folder and then put the folder in a large, blank brown envelope.

"Are you going to wait for him at the coffee shop? I think he would like to talk to you."

"Yes, I'll wait. Just text me when he shows up."

"I will. I don't why he's late. He's usually very timely, and he had everything done as of last night."

"That's okay," Clint said and left.

The summaries of the documents along with their historical significance Forthsyte had provided impressed Clint. Forthsyte and whoever he contacted definitely knew a lot about Las Vegas' past.

The two checks looked in order and, for some reason, had Clint feeling a little guilty. Despite over a century of abandonment, he had a sense that he was taking someone else's money. The feeling didn't last long. The checks reflected the Forthsyte Law Office as the payor, which was in synch with Clint's request that the buyer not know who he was. Paranoid or not, he thought it wiser to keep his identity known only to the law office where it could be kept confidential.

He glanced back at the receipts and reread the legalese at the bottom of the page. Melanie's calling it mumbo-jumbo was right. The narrative did its best to say that with his signing of the receipt he acknowledged that just about anything that could go wrong would not be considered the lawyer's fault.

Clint's cell phone said it was forty minutes past two. He sent a text to Melanie asking if she had heard anything. As he waited for a response, he started to get an uneasy feeling. He got up and started walking back to the law office. He skipped the elevator and jogged up the three flights of stairs.

He turned the knob, and the door swung open without making a noise. Across the room, he saw a man holding Melanie from behind with something pressed against her head.

"Where is it?" the man shouted. Fortunately, both the man and Melanie faced way from Clint, looking into Forthsyte's office.

"I told you, either Mr. Forthsyte has it, or it's in his safe," Melanie sobbed.

Clint wished he hadn't left his Beretta in his car, but he also knew he had to do something fast. He took five rapid steps and drove his fist as hard as he could into the back of the man's neck. The man collapsed to the floor, and Clint grabbed Melanie.

"Now," he ordered and tugged Melanie by the arm. They both raced for the door and crossed through it as something ripped into the door frame a split second after they were through. "Quick, to the stairs."

They reached the stairs and Clint glanced behind them as they entered the stairwell and the door to the hallway closed. He saw no one.

Melanie clung to his arm, still shaking from the experience. Her bottom lip was swollen and bloody, "They wanted your land deed. Why would they want it?" She talked fast and her voice trembled.

"I have no idea. Let's go upstairs. I don't want to go downstairs and find someone waiting for us," Clint said.

"They said they were going to rape me and then kill me if I didn't tell them where the deed was. I would've told them, but I don't know what he did with them."

Clint had to pull Melanie by the hand to get her moving. "You know, he didn't give me a copy, either. I thought they might be in the folder, but neither were in the folder you gave me this morning."

"Then he would've given you a copy when he saw you."

They entered the fourth floor.

"Are you friends with anyone up here? We need to call the police."

"There," Melanie pointed to door with a plaque that read Canyon Title Inc. "I'm friends with Suzi."

"Let's get in there and call the police. She can keep you hidden, too, until the police arrive. And Melanie, I need you to keep the details of my involvement with your office confidential. Privileged information, right?"

She nodded, "Of course."

"If whoever is looking for the deed knows I'm the one who brought it to Forthsyte, they may believe I have a copy or the original. They will come after me."

Her eyes widened. "That's right."

They entered the offices of Canyon Title. A very cute brunette that Clint guessed to be in her mid-thirties sat behind the reception desk.

"Melanie, what's the matter?" the woman stood and rushed around the desk to us. She stopped at the last second and looked at Clint.

"I didn't do it, but we need to use your phone to call the police right now," I said.

"Suzi, I'll explain," she said, reaching over the desk to the office phone. She picked it up and dialed 911. Her explanation to Suzi came indirectly, as Melanie told the story to the police on the phone. "Yes, I believe I am safe now, but I don't know if the men are still in my office. Yes, I'll stay here until someone calls me back and says it's safe to come down."

After she hung up, she took my hand again and said, "Clint saved me. I think they were going to kill me."

Suzi studied me again, "Thank you for rescuing my friend. Was that a gunshot I heard a minute ago?"

"Yes, and I kind of had no choice but to help Melanie," Clint said. Suzi reminded him of a movie star or other celebrity, but he couldn't place who.

She took Melanie's arm and walked her over to a couch, where they both sat down.

"Do you mind?" Clint asked and locked the door to the hallway. "I don't believe they will come up here looking for her, but it's a simple precaution."

"Better yet, why don't you two wait in the break room. That way if someone knocks, and I open the door, they won't see you," Suzi said.

Clint felt like saying just don't open the door, but he followed Melanie and Suzi into the small break room. "You're welcome to the coffee or anything you can find in the fridge," she said. "Suzi, have you called your boss and told him what happened?"

"He has a message to call me, but my phone and purse are still downstairs."

"Want me to go get it?" Suzi asked.

"No!" Suzi said. "The men might still be there."

"Surely they're gone by now, and I don't see why they would bother me," Suzi said.

"The police should be here any second, so I suggest we all wait here until they do," Clint said.

"Okay. Well, let me go sit at my desk. That way I can hear if someone knocks on the door."

"That's fine, Suzi, and thank you again," Melanie said.

Clint watched her walk out of the breakroom.

"Beautiful, isn't she?" Melanie asked as though she was reading my mind.

"I hadn't noticed," Clint grinned.

"Well, notice the big ring on her finger."

Clint smiled again, wondering why Melanie made the remark. He saw that her left hand was ringless.

CHAPTER 6

Two uniformed and two plain clothes police officers occupied the Forthsyte Law Office when Melanie and Clint returned to it. She had received a call from the police, telling her it was all clear and that she should come back to the office. The older looking officer in a faded, grey suit instructed Clint to wait outside the door as Melanie took them through the office.

A young patrol officer stood by the door, guarding the entrance to the office and trying to ignore Clint.

"Did you notice that?" Clint asked and pointed to the hole in the door frame about head high.

The cop looked at it and then back at Clint. "Is that a bullet hole?"

"Yep. One of the guys who busted the place up took a shot at us as we were running out. Point it out to the detective. He'll be impressed with your observation skills, and I won't tell him I mentioned it to you."

"I'll do that, thanks." His look lingered on Clint as if to ask why.

"No need to thank me. Next time, you'll find the bullet hole on your own."

"I will," he said. "Were you a cop?"

"No, military."

The young police officer nodded.

They waited in silence for a few minutes until the older detective came to the door.

"Detective Yates did you see this?" The young cop pointed to the bullet hole.

"What do we have here?" Yates asked.

"When Melanie and I ran out of the office, one of the men shot at us. I thought I heard an impact, so," Clint walked up to the hole in the door frame as though he was seeing the hole for the first time, "this is where it must have hit the wall."

"Good eye, Mick," the older detective said to the young cop. The young officer beamed at the compliment.

"Thank you, sir."

"Mr. Smith? Right?" Detective Yates asked Clint.

"That's me, and it's my real name."

"Come on in. We need to talk."

Clint followed Yates into the office. Yates sat on the edge of Melanie's desk.

"Ms. Schell said you rescued her today. What brought you here, and what did you see when you entered the room?"

"I had an appointment with her boss at two o'clock--"

"Two? Why were you late?"

"I arrived at two, but he wasn't here. I waited here with Melanie for a few minutes, and then at her suggestion, I went to the coffee shop next door to continue my wait. I never heard from her, and when she didn't return my text, I decided to come back here."

Yates nodded but didn't take any notes. "What happened when you got back?"

"I walked into the office and saw a man with short black hair and wearing a dark, untucked shirt holding Melanie by the back of the neck and pressing something metallic against the side of her head. I didn't see it well, just a flash of metal, but I thought it was a knife. They both faced into Forthsyte's office and didn't see me."

"Why didn't you just turn around and leave?"

"I was already in the room, and, well, I pretty much reacted by instinct. I hit the back of the man's neck as hard as I could. He collapsed to the ground, and I pulled Melanie out of the office."

"Pulled?" Yates asked.

"She needed a little encouragement to move, and I knew we didn't have much time."

"Brave but stupid. You're lucky the other man had his head down, looking into the lawyer's desk."

"I did realize that later, when he shot at us."

"Did you get a look at either man?" Yates asked.

"Only the back view of the one. He's about five foot ten, more than likely right-handed based on how he was holding something and threatening Melanie."

"How well do you know Melanie?"

"Not at all, I've only had contact with her a couple times and only in relationship with my business with her boss."

"And that business is?"

"Sorry, but you know I don't have to tell you that," Clint said and saw Yates' demeanor harden for a second.

"Did it have anything to do with this?"

Clint had expected this question. "You'll have to ask Forthsyte that question, but I have no knowledge of what could have motivated anyone to come in here and do this. My business with Forthsyte was purely personal and was not related to any other individuals or businesses. I came to him because my privacy in this matter is very important to me. He can better explain to you what he did for me."

"Do you know where he might be?"

"No. I do know that Melanie has been trying to contact him."

"You in the military?" Yates asked.

"Was."

"Thought so. Most civilians wouldn't have done what you did or know how to put a man down with one punch. I don't mean to give you a hard time. It's just, you know, you're here when all this goes down."

Clint nodded. Melanie and the other two policemen walked out of Forthsyte's office.

"Bert," the other detective addressed Yates. "Nothing appears to be missing, but someone has definitely gone through the files. Trashed the place."

"Figures," Yates said.

Clint heard some people approaching in the hallway and turned to see two women arrive. One had a police credentials hanging from her belt. He assumed the other one had hers in a pocket. They both carried small, black briefcases and wore what looked like matching black suits.

"Hey, Yates, what do we have today?" the woman with no visible badge or credentials asked.

"Besides that, Doc," Yates pointed toward the bullet hole on the door frame, "pretty much a standard burglary attempt."

"You okay?" Doc asked Melanie, seeing her bruised lip.

"Oh, yeah. One of the guys smacked her in the face," Yates said as though he had seen so many similar situations of physical assault that this one barely warranted mentioning.

"You okay?" Doc repeated.

"Yes. I was more terrified than injured," Melanie said.

"If you're done here," she addressed Yates, "how about letting Jeri and me see what we can find."

"All yours," Yates said. "I'll leave Mick here, so you won't be disturbed." Out in the hallway, Yates stopped, causing the five to cluster together. "Smith, you didn't get a look at either of the two, right?"

"That's right."

"Ernie, get his number and where he's staying and let him go. Ms. Schell, I need you to come with me to the station for a few final things. You're in no trouble at all, it's just that we need to formalize a few things and get a better picture of what these two guys looked like."

"Okay," she said.

"I'll wait for you downstairs, Ernie," Yates said.

Clint gave the info to Ernie, and he jotted it down on a small paper tablet. He had to fight the urge to ask him if the two of them, Bert and Ernie, got ribbed about being a team.

Ernie hurried down the stairs and the other uniformed police officer drifted back to be with his partner by the door.

Clint didn't feel good about any of this.

CHAPTER 7

"Bert, it's Forthsyte, alright. We'll have to get someone to confirm it, but he looks just like he does on his website. A little less healthy, though," Ernie said.

Detective Yates looked over at the small crowd about ten yards away made up of county crime scene investigators and law enforcement personnel from a variety of jurisdictions. Yates had already taken a look at the body. Someone had beaten Forthsyte, causing the bruising to his face, and had mangled his hand, perhaps with a pair of plyers. Death, Yates believed, came from a single bullet wound to the chest.

Neither Bert or Ernie worked homicide, but this was related to their investigation. They had only released Ms. Melanie Schell about an hour before this call came in.

"Looks like they were trying to get some information out of him before they killed him. Think he held out?" Ernie asked.

"Why would he? We're not talking national secrets here. No, I bet he spilled everything he knew the first time they, if it was a they, broke a finger. They either thought he knew more than he did, or someone just enjoyed doing that to him."

"I wonder what they would've done to Ms. Schell?"

"Don't even go there, Ernie. Imagining things that could've happened won't help us now or ever. Did you hear anything about an estimated time of death?"

"Just a few hours ago. We got lucky, a bicycle club used this access road on their route today, and one of the riders spotted the body. If they hadn't been out here, the body probably wouldn't have been found for a few days."

"I know." Yates looked around the dry desolate terrain. "You think they always ride this far out of the city?"

"Dunno. Can't see how either Ms. Schell or that Mr. Smith could have done this. I can't believe Ms. Schell had any knowledge of this happening today, either," Ernie said.

"I agree. Makes no sense. I don't see Smith involved with this either. Why would he interrupt the search, and why would they shoot at him if he was one of them?"

"That's right. What do you think our role will be in this homicide investigation? I haven't worked a homicide yet."

"Hold that thought," Yates said. "Your answer may be coming right now."

Ernie looked behind him and saw the lead homicide investigator approaching. The man walked hunched over slightly and looked even older than Yates. His grey, balding hair added to that impression.

"Bert, this is your missing guy. No wallet on him, but it's him. You two have a jump on us on this one, so I'm going to ask the Lieutenant to let us team up for the rest of this investigation. Is that alright with you?"

"Yeah, it's fine by us, Willard."

A few minutes later, Yates steered the police issued, unmarked Ford back toward the city of Las Vegas.

"This will be my first homicide," Ernie said.

"Keep wearing that badge, and it won't be your last. You have that girl's address?" Yates asked.

"I think so." Ernie fumbled through his pockets until he found his note pad. "Yes, she lives in the city. We're going there?"

"After we get something to eat. First, we need to find out if someone's notified the lawyer's next of kin before we talk to her, because I don't want to beat around the bush when we do talk to her. And Ernie…."

"Yes."

"Call and confirm we have someone keeping an eye on her place."

"Think she's in danger?"

Yates glanced at him. "Come on, Ernie. Someone violently killed her boss today and then assaulted her while ransacking her office. Did you notice what she didn't say about the two men in her office today?"

"You mean their descriptions?"

"They weren't wearing masks. They had killed one man and went into that office without taking the time to cover their faces."

"They were going to kill her, too. Bert, don't you think we should make sure the unit watching her place knows about this."

"They shouldn't need the warning, but yes, it couldn't hurt. When you verify someone is still there, ask them to give the guy a heads up on the murder, too."

Ernie made the call. After he ended the call, he said, "Someone is posted outside her apartment, and they'll update her on the latest. Her being the cop."

"Yeah, I heard. This good?" Yates asked as he pulled into a Denny's parking lot.

"Fine," Ernie replied, wondering why Yates always asked that question after they were in the parking lot. He didn't mind Denny's, but he wouldn't go there by choice. Yates almost never ate anywhere else.

Yates ordered the spaghetti dinner, and Ernie asked for a hamburger.

"We'll need to press a lot harder now."

"On the woman, Bert?"

"Unless you know someone else to press harder on. She referred to the men asking about a deed. We need to get a copy of that deed."

"She said that Forthsyte may have taken the deed with him. She didn't find it in the office."

"Only means she didn't find a copy during a quick search while she was under duress. She may remember something else now."

"I don't think she was holding back on us."

"We'll see," Yates said.

CHAPTER 8

"Buzz, I'm going to send you pictures of two old property deeds. They're something I found out here. Quality may not be too good, as I took them before I gave them to a lawyer here. Can you check them out and tell me where the land is, and what if any significance it might have?"

"Can't you have someone out there do this quicker than I can? I mean, it's not something that falls under our area of expertise," Buzz said. His voice came through the phone loud and clear.

"I know, but you wanted me to keep a low profile, and someone has already been assaulted over one of these deeds."

"What? My suggestion is to throw the deeds in the trash and get out of town today."

"Can't do that. Already had my chat with the police, and they have little interest in me, but if I skip town that may change. If I go to someone local, I just put that person in danger."

"Okay, send me the deeds. I'll see what I can do."

"Thanks, Buzz." Clint ended the call and checked his phone. He had a phone message from Melanie, asking him to call her.

He looked at the time on his phone. Eight thirty, not too late to call her back, he thought.

"Clint," she sounded like she had been crying. "Oh, Clint, they killed him. They killed him."

"Forthsyte? He's dead?"

"Yes. I'm scared, they have a policewoman guarding my front door, but I'm scared. Can you come over and stay with me for a while?"

"Sure, but they shouldn't have a reason to come after you. They already searched your office," Clint said.

"Please."

"Okay, I'll be right over, but, where are you?"

She lived in a large apartment complex, not far from downtown. Clint took the stairs to the third floor and then had to follow a few arrows listing apartment numbers to get to her apartment. He spotted a woman in a Las Vegas city police uniform sitting in a chair in the hallway. She looked up at Clint as he approached.

"Good evening," Clint said.

"Evening, are you Clint?" The police woman stood up. She was almost as tall as Clint. "She's waiting for you," she said, after he admitted he was. She nodded to the door directly in front of her.

Clint knocked and within a couple of seconds, Melanie opened the door.

"Are you okay?" Clint asked once they were inside.

"Yes. I think I've calmed down a little since they told me, but I'm still glad you're here. I can't believe this is really happening." She was wearing dark blue yoga pants and a white tee shirt.

"It doesn't make sense to me either, Melanie. Those deeds are well over a hundred years old. There has to be some other explanation."

"This whole thing is ridiculous. Please sit down. Can I get you a beer or something?"

"A beer will be fine."

Melanie disappeared into the kitchen for a moment before reappearing with two bottles of Michelob Ultra. "Is this okay? I try to keep the carbs down."

"That's fine. Did your boss say anything at all about the two deeds? I mean there were two. Do we even know which one the men were after?"

"No." Melanie sat back on large stuffed chair and closed her eyes. She opened them and shook her head gently. "There were two deeds. That's right. They came looking for just one. Everything has been about one deed. I don't think I even told the police there were two of them."

"You can't recall anything they may have said that would indicate which deed they wanted?"

"No, but the only ones I know he has had in a long time were the ones you brought in. He doesn't do real estate law. It would've had to have been one of the two you gave him, but I have no idea which one."

"Well, we have to provide copies of both to the police. Maybe they can dig something up," Clint said.

"We should. I haven't told them anything about you, other than you are a client, and that you saved me from those two. But I thought you wanted to stay anonymous."

"Hardly am anymore. What I'd like to do is give you copies and have you hand them to the police. Without giving them my name, tell them the truth about how the documents came to your office, my story about the discovery of all the documents, and Forthsyte's role in selling them to a museum. When you give them the copy of the two deeds, ensure the cops understand that these two weren't up for sale. The deeds were going to be handed over to the county or state land office, or whatever is the right place where title and deeds are kept. If you can find copies of the summaries that you gave me, give them those, too. None of the documents had my name on them, and I would still like to stay as much out of it as possible. I know that may ultimately be impossible."

"I don't remember seeing the summaries, but we must have them, so I should be able to make copies of all the summaries," she said

"Good, they didn't ask for those today from you, so they can't get too upset at you holding anything back. Please, don't give them copies of the receipts or anything regarding the coins."

"Can you tell me why you don't want to just come out and let them know you're the client behind all this? You didn't do anything wrong."

"I have a sensitive job, and I'm already on thin ice. My bosses hate publicity, especially bad publicity, or anything that might cause scrutiny by the press. Believe me, I'm not into anything illegal."

"Okay. Even though he's dead, I think I still have a responsibility to follow your instructions."

"Did he have a family?" Clint asked.

"Yes, a wife, two sons who have families of their own. They'll be crushed." Melanie's eyes started filling with tears again.

"Yeah, this whole thing sucks. All over my little buried treasure. I should've left it alone." Clint leaned back on the couch and took a long drink of beer.

"Don't blame yourself. Forthsyte thought the stuff you

found was fascinating, and he loved going to his friends to share them. Between you and me, he did say he could've gotten you more for the documents, but he said you weren't after top dollar."

"He's right. The money was never important."

They talked for a while about what Melanie planned on doing now that she faced unemployment. She didn't know.

"Let me see if I can get Frankie a cup of coffee or something," Melanie said and went to the front door. She opened it and briefly talked to the policewoman in the hall. "She says she's fine. Don't you think she's pretty?"

"Yes, but I only saw her for a second."

"She's tall, beautiful eyes, and in really great physical shape. She says she works out every day. I'd love to be tall like her, and her hair. You know she said she's part Hawaiian."

"We all should work out more," Clint said. "You look in great shape, too."

She smiled, and their conversation slowly digressed. Clint finally decided it was time to leave when Melanie untangled herself from Clint on the couch.

"Oh, Clint, I want you to stay, but it isn't right. He just died. I can't be doing this." She lowered herself back on Clint and kissed him again. Her body language seemed to be ignoring her own words. "Oh, Clint."

He pushed her gently off him and stood up. "Hey, it's alright. We can see each other tomorrow."

"Are you mad? Don't be mad." She took a step toward him and reached out like she wanted to embrace him again.

Clint put both hands on her shoulders and stopped her. "I'm not mad. I didn't come over here with any expectations other than to make sure you were okay and had someone to talk to. We can continue this tomorrow if you would like. Maybe we could go up to the dam and rent a boat or something. A lot has already happened today."

"Okay, you're right. I would like to go out with you tomorrow."

"I'll give you a call in the morning," Clint said.

She nodded and smiled. "You're not mad?"

"No. We'll have time together tomorrow." He left the apartment, closing the door behind him. Frankie stood up, looking tired. "Hope someone's coming to replace you before it gets too late."

"It's late already, but someone should be here soon."

"Well, take care. I hope it's a quiet night," Clint said and left. He couldn't help to think that Melanie's remark that Frankie was pretty might have been a bit of an understatement.

CHAPTER 9

Clint went for a long run in the morning before showering and having a late breakfast. He called Melanie at ten thirty and was surprised when a man answered the phone.

"Hello," the man said.

"Is Melanie there?"

"She can't come to the phone right now. May I say who's calling?"

"Sure, tell her Clint called."

Client broke the call and immediately dialed the number on the card Ernie had given him the previous day. When he answered, Clint interrupted him, "Ernie, listen, I think Melanie is in trouble. I just called her and a man answered. He said she was unavailable. Could someone check on her right away."

"We can certainly do that, Mr. Smith. Where are you right now?"

"At my hotel, The Orleans."

"One second," Ernie said.

Clint could tell he was having a conversation with someone but couldn't make out what was being said.

"We'll follow up on Ms. Schell, but we want someone to come to you, so we can follow up with a couple things with you, too. Can you be in the lobby in fifteen minutes?"

"Yes." The call ended. Clint felt like something wasn't right, and it only took a few seconds to realize what was bothering him. Ernie's voice lacked any anxiety, like he wasn't worried for Melanie. Maybe the police were already on top of the situation, but wouldn't he have said something to that effect?

He was tempted to call back, but decided to go to the lobby and wait for the police to arrive. He would get his answers then. The wait turned out to be twenty minutes, and Clint was surprised to see Frankie, the police woman from the night before, enter the Orleans accompanied by another police officer in uniform. She saw him and came straight to him with her partner trying to keep up with her.

Clint smiled and nodded at her as she approached, but he didn't see a hint of happiness in her eyes.

"Mr. Smith, this is Officer Higgins. We need to ask you a few questions."

"Frankie, did they not give you my message? Some man answered Melanie's phone this morning and wouldn't put her on. You need to have someone check on her."

"We need you to answer a couple of our questions first," Officer Higgins said. He looked to be in his early thirties, medium build with short black hair. He looked far too serious.

Clint stared at Higgins, and things started to fall into place. He looked into Frankie's eyes and could read the bad news.

She gave him an almost imperceptible nod.

"Mr. Smith," Higgins said. "Where have you…"

Frankie touched her partners arm, "It's alright, Jimmy. We can tell him first."

Clint didn't need to be told. "After I left you, I came straight back here and have not left since. I did go for a run this morning, but that's all. I imagine most all of that can be verified by the hotel's security cameras."

"Thanks, we'll need to verify that," Frankie said. "Someone killed both Melanie and one of our officers last night."

"They took their time with her," Higgins said.

Frankie gave Higgins a look that did little to hide her displeasure in his remark. "We need to get to the bottom of this and soon," Frankie said.

"I can see I'm going to be a suspect in this until you can verify that I was here," Clint said and turned his face to look at Higgins. "Why don't you go and check with hotel security and verify when I went into my room last night and when I left. They should have me leaving on my run this morning, too."

"Why don't you...." Higgins started to say when Frankie cut him off.

"No, Jimmy, that's actually a good idea. Go check with security."

Higgins didn't look happy, but he stood up and started to leave.

"I'm in room 8034," Clint said as the officer left them.

"Don't mind Jimmy. He's a good cop. He just has a habit of thinking everyone is guilty until proven innocent."

"What happened?" Clint asked.

"We don't know much yet. It happened between two and four this morning. We have a lot of people working it. We'll find out."

"I imagine you're here to eliminate me as a suspect."

"Partially, I don't think anyone is looking at you as a suspect. I know someone will want to interview you again."

"Isn't that why you are here?"

"I don't mean to worry you, but Detective Yates thinks you might be next."

"Next?" Clint said, but the possibility had already crossed his mind. In fact, he had to hold himself back from saying I hope so.

"Yes, but if you don't mind, I'll spend the day here with you. You'll be safe."

Clint sat back and took a deep breath.

Frankie took this as a sign that Clint was worried. "I'm good at what I do. Everything should be fine."

"I know it will be. I just don't want you to get hurt."

She smiled, "That's nice, but it's my job."

"What's your partner's role in all this?"

Frankie's eyes darkened, and she frowned before she realized to whom Clint was referring. "You mean Jimmy? He's not my partner. We go back to the academy together, but he was just at the scene and drove me here. He's not staying."

"Was it your partner last night?"

"Yes," Frankie said.

"Sorry. I guess that makes it personal for both of us."

Frankie started to say something but didn't.

"Let me buy you a cup of coffee or something to eat," Clint said. "We have to wait for Jimmy anyway, and I have something to discuss with you."

The café was still serving breakfast. Frankie ordered coffee and toast, so Clint, despite having just eaten, ordered the same.

"Can you get Detective Yates to come over here. I'd rather talk to him and you, and I'd rather do it here."

"I can ask, Clint, but what do you know that you haven't already told us?"

"Don't get upset."

"My partner, my friend, was murdered last night, and now you're telling me you've held out on us?" Her glare became intense, and Clint imagined she wanted to reach over and smack him.

"Melanie didn't lie when she said the men who invaded her office were looking for a deed. She didn't know why it was important to them and had no reason to believe that the other documents she had might have any significance at all. Today she was going to give you everything related."

"Related?"

"Everything else the client brought in for the lawyer to examine."

"That client was you," Frankie said.

"Yes, and as you know the business conducted between a client and his lawyer is confidential. That caused her hesitancy. Once she found out Forthsyte was murdered, she wanted to turn everything over. That's why she asked me to come over last night. I told her it was alright. She would have given you everything this morning."

"What is it?"

"Just some very old documents. I found a buried treasure. Not really, a buried stage coach strong box. It contained several documents, and while none of them seemed important, they were really old. Forthsyte is tight with a bunch of historical groups, so I asked him to see if a museum might be interested in them. He had my permission to sell them cheap, but I wanted a summary of what each document was."

"Weren't they in English?"

"Yes, but most of them referred to places or incidents that I didn't recognize. One was a list of provisions, half of which I didn't even know what they were. It was just curiosity. I didn't need the summaries prior to his selling the documents."

"And these guys are after one of those documents?"

"Not those," Clint said. "Along with these documents, I found two land deeds. Forthsyte said these should be filed with some state land office as historical records. I said fine. I think, but I don't know for sure, that he was out yesterday morning trying to learn more about those deeds."

"And that struck a nerve."

"A big one apparently."

"Do you have any of these documents?" Frankie asked.

"I have the summaries of the ones Forthsyte sold to some museum. I do have pictures of the two deeds. Forthsyte said for me to hold onto the original of the deeds, as he wasn't selling them, but I told him he could hang onto them. I never intended to keep them. Once he determined what they were for, we could give them to whatever office would like them."

"Where are they now?"

"In my car."

"Can we get them now?"

"Yes, and no offense, but I want to talk to Yates. I really don't want my name to get leaked out to the press. I'd like to get some reassurance."

"If you're afraid of these men coming after you, I'm afraid Melanie may have given you up," Frankie said.

Again, Clint almost said that he actually wanted these men to come after him, but then realized as someone under witness protection, his name could be protected better than any other way.

"We can go get the stuff out of my car now."

"Let me call Detective Yates first." She did, and when the call ended, the two stood up and walked out of the hotel café.

"He'll be here within the hour, guess he's still out at the

crime scene."

The late morning sun felt good after leaving the airconditioned building.

"A bad crime scene?" Clint asked.

"Yes."

They walked in silence until Clint clicked his key fob and the Lincoln's lights flashed on. They could hear the click of the locks releasing.

"Nice car," Frankie said.

Clint slid into the driver's seat and reached for the envelope stuffed down between the passenger seat and the console panel. His eyes caught movement in the rearview mirror. He looked into the mirror and saw two men remove pistols from under their shirts as they approached the back of his car.

"Down" he shouted.

Frankie had stopped in front of the car and had her back to the men. At Clint's command she dropped to a squatting position and spun around, drawing her service weapon when she saw the men.

Clint grabbed his 9mm from its concealed spot in the car. Staying in the car, he twisted his body around and leaned out far enough to get an aim. The two men started shooting and both Frankie and Clint returned fire. Both men fell to the ground.

"Are you okay?" Clint shouted, keeping his eyes on the two men.

"Yes, your car door gave me cover."

Clint glanced at the door and saw three holes in the interior panel. "Damn." He got out of the car and started to close the door when he saw a third man running at them in front of the car with a handgun of some type aimed at them. The man fired and Clint fired back, feeling a sting in his left arm as he did.

Frankie spun around as the man collapsed to the ground between two parked cars in the row in front of them. "Watch those two," Frankie said, pointing at the two men behind the car. She jogged over to the third man on the pavement. She looked up at Clint and shook her head.

Clint took a couple of steps toward the two men about five yards behind the car then stopped, hearing the roar of a heavy engine. He looked and saw a black SUV racing toward them with a man leaning out the front passenger window with what looked like an AR-15.

"In the car, quick!"

Frankie heard him and raced to the passenger door. Clint jumped into the driver's seat and as soon as Frankie climbed in, he gunned the engine, and the MKZ shot out of the spot and away from the oncoming SUV. The rear window exploded and loud pops could be heard as rounds from the AR smacked into the trunk of the car.

With the rear window gone, Frankie spun around and fired off three rounds at the SUV. One of the rounds must have struck the vehicle and perhaps someone in it. The SUV swerved and slowed before the driver restarted the chase. The few seconds hesitation allowed Clint to turn right onto Tropicana Avenue about ten seconds before the SUV. A traffic light must have changed behind him as a steady row of cars forced the SUV to stop before it could get out of the parking lot.

Clint took advantage of the time, flooring the accelerator of the MKZ.

"You okay?" Clint asked.

"Yes," Frankie replied and started talking into her phone.

Clint slowed enough to take a left on a street that was significant enough to warrant a stop light on Tropicana. He hoped the light would be red by the time the SUV got to it and that the men in the SUV didn't see him make the turn.

He slowed down to just a few miles per hour over the speed limit. Frankie was doing her best to explain what had just happened to someone who had a lot of questions. She glanced around and looked behind them. "Yes, I think we've lost them. We'll turn around in a minute and head back to the hotel."

"Can you believe he was more concerned about why we left the crime scene than if we were okay?" she said after the call ended.

"You can blame that on me. Tell them I panicked."

"We had no choice. There were four men in that SUV. All of them may have had us outgunned."

They drove through an industrial area that looked abandoned as Clint searched for a good spot where he could make a U-turn. His phone buzzed, grabbing it, he looked at the text on the screen. "You or your car has a tracking device on it."

"Not good," he muttered to himself and turned up a side street before coming to a stop. He jumped out of the car and started looking for anything attached to it that shouldn't be there.

Frankie got out and asked, "What are you doing?"

"Looking for a tracking device. See if you can find it." He squatted and looked along the undercarriage. "It should be somewhere easily accessible."

"Why do you think – oh here's something." Frankie

unattached a small metallic box from under the passenger side front wheel well. "How the hell did you know?"

"It's not yours?"

"No, how do you open it?"

Clint didn't get a chance to answer as the black SUV raced around the corner barely fifty yards away.

"Quick over the wall!" Clint yelled as he jumped over an adjacent four-foot high, concrete, cinder block wall and onto the parking lot of an abandoned warehouse.

Frankie cleared the wall a second later, and both took firing positions as the SUV skidded to a stop. Three men and a woman came out firing automatic weapons. Clint and Frankie returned fire, but in seconds there was so much dust and concrete fragments in the air in front of them they had to move. Clint ducked low and ran about ten yards to his left before he raised high enough to fire again over the wall. As he did, the automatic weapons began to shred the wall in front of him, allowing Frankie to resume firing.

The firefight lasted less than twenty seconds. Clint stood and looked at the four bodies on the ground. None of them moved or showed any sign of life.

"We were lucky the wall was here," Frankie said, approaching him. Her face was bleeding from a couple of gashes.

"That's why I parked here. Are you okay?"

"Caught some fragments from the wall in my face," she said. Clint had to give her credit; she didn't reach up to check out the injuries. "Let's make sure they stay down." She jumped over the wall and walked up to the bodies on the ground. "I thought they were all men."

"Looks like gang members like the ones back in the parking lot. They all have the tats, and none of them are going anywhere."

"Except this one," Frankie said, looking at a body in front of the SUV. "No tats and looks Asian. He doesn't fit."

Clint joined her and leaned down to look at the man. "You should probably call this in."

"God, I'll be on desk duty for the rest of my life." She reached for her phone, but it wasn't on her person. "It's in the car," she said and walked over to the Lincoln. Clint took out his phone and snapped a picture of the Asian man. He sent it to Buzz with a question mark.

"Oh no, no! My life sucks!" Frankie shouted from the car.

Clint looked over and saw additional damage to his car. Frankie held up a shattered cell phone. She sat down on the ground, and Clint saw her whole body begin to shake.

"Hey, hey," he said, rushing over and helping her to her feet. "Sit down in the car and relax your breathing. You're going into shock or at least a severe adrenalin high." He buckled her into the seat and went around, getting into the driver's seat. "If no reinforcements are coming, we need to get out of here."

He drove away from the city for about five miles before pulling behind a deserted gas station. Two old wooden buildings that may have been businesses at one time stood vacant nearby. Frankie hadn't said a thing, but at one point she had looked over at Clint and smiled. With the car stopped, he reached behind his seat and grabbed a bottle of water for Frankie.

"Drink a little," he said.

She did. "I don't understand any of this. Why would the Demons, I believe that's the gang they are in, have any interest in any of this, and why would an Asian man be involved with them?"

"A foreign exchange gang member?"

"You're not serious."

"No," Clint said. "Are you okay?"

"Yes, I just felt sick and dizzy for a minute. A lot has happened today. I've never been in a shootout before. Now I've been involved in two, and I've lost a partner." She shook her head and stared at Clint. "You're bleeding," she said, reaching over and lifted Clint's left arm.

"A graze from the attack in the parking lot at the hotel. It's nothing, but let me get my first aid kit, and we can fix each other up."

CHAPTER 10

"Your first aid kit is a little more extensive than the ones I've seen before, and you handle a weapon well," Frankie said. She finished wrapping a bandage around the wound on his arm. "Who are you?"

They both leaned against the front of the car, the late morning sun beating down on them.

"One of the good guys, and I honestly have no idea what is going on here."

"No, I mean is Clint Smith really your name? It sounds barely better than John Doe."

"Yes, it's my name."

"You have a license for that Beretta?"

"Yes, it's legit."

"Back there, how did you know to look for a tracking device on the car?" Frankie asked.

"There is going to be some information about me I'm not going to be able to tell you, Frankie. But everything about anything I know about what's going on here and my involvement, I can and will be honest about." He pulled the gold coin out of his pocket, and flipped it to her.

She caught it and stared at it. "This is gold, right? What are you trying to bribe me?"

Clint laughed, "No, I want that back, but it's about the only thing about this whole mess I haven't talked about. When I found the strong box, there were close to twenty coins like that one in it."

"Where are the rest?"

"Forthsyte sold them for me. It's all in that envelope I was trying to hand to you. There's no way the coins are involved, though. Can't be. Has to have something to do with one of the deeds, but why a land deed from a hundred plus years ago has any relevance today is beyond me."

Frankie handed him the coin. "Where's the envelope?"

"I hope still in the car, under the passenger seat."

She walked to the car, and after opening the passenger door, returned with the envelope in hand. "Can I?" she asked.

"Sure. Read to your hearts content. I need to make a call? He walked over to the side of the building and called Section. Deer answered.

"Not what I call a low profile, Clint," Deer said. "What the hell is going on?"

"You probably know more than I do right now?"

"That's normally the case. You have Buzz all spun up. You know I can't operate without him, and you are always getting him stressed out."

"Anything I need to know?"

"Soon. I need you to lay low for a day, maybe two. We're sending you coordinates for a bed and breakfast not far from you. We've booked you and paid for two nights. This thing you stumbled into may be big." Deer didn't usually call things big.

"I may have one complication. I have a police officer with me."

"Are you under arrest?"

"No, nothing like that. In fact, we've been supporting each other in a couple of rough spots."

"A her?"

"Yes."

"Well, take her with you or leave her there, but you need to move now. As you know, the city and the county are going crazy over all this."

Clint didn't know, but it didn't surprise him either. "Ok, I'll be out of here soon."

He walked back to the car. Frankie was still reading the documents but looked up as he approached. "There's nothing here."

"Welcome to my world. Forthsyte was the expert on this old stuff, and he didn't see anything there either, except that it was old and therefore might be of interest to a museum. Melanie was as confused as we are."

"I need to get these to our experts."

"That's fine, Frankie, but I need you to make a quick decision. I'm leaving in a minute to find a spot to maintain a low profile for a couple of days. I'm not leaving the area. You are welcome to stay here, and we'll call in so someone can come get you. Or you can come with me. We can still call it in."

"You can't just leave. There's a pile of bodies we've left behind. We can't just leave them."

"I'm going to call Detective Yates and tell him to come get you, but if you want to see this through to the end and keep me safe, you'll be coming with me. I'll remain in your protective custody but at a location you need to promise me you'll keep to yourself."

"That's not fair," Frankie said.

Clint called Yates.

"Hello, who's this?" Yates said into the phone.

"It's Clint. Frankie and I are ok. A few scratches but we're okay. They knew where I was and had a tracking device on my car. I'm going to hide out for a few days, until you have this under control, but I'll be back. I've given Frankie the choice to come with me if she would like to. Yes, here she is." Clint gave his phone to her.

"Yes, I'm fine. No, no, no. Yes. Are you sure? Yes, I think so. Okay." She handed the phone back to Clint.

"I guess I'm going with you."

"Then let's move."

Clint drove further away from Las Vegas and up one of the several mountain sides to a small town. The two had ridden in silence for fifteen minutes.

"Who programmed your nav settings?" Frankie asked as they entered the town and took a right turn.

"With all the damage done to the car, I'm surprised the nav system still works. I had it programmed earlier as a possible place to stay when I got to Vegas." Clint doubted she believed him. "You know we were lucky back there. If they weren't so gung-ho to jump out of their vehicle firing in full-automatic, they wouldn't have been such easy targets."

"I know, we were lucky," Frankie said.

"What do you think is going on?"

"Me? I have no idea. I'm starting to believe I'm protecting a man who needs less protection than I do for reasons and from whom I don't understand."

"Look at the next couple of days as a vacation. You're probably overdue one," Clint said.

"Don't smile at me. I'm not at all happy with the way this is going."

Clint stopped the car in front of a building that faced Las

Vegas, which was now below them in the distance. A sign identified the place as The Clipper, a modern B&B with style.

"Why here?" Frankie asked. She got out of the car and looked around. The road they came up on seemed to die a few hundred yards away at the far edge of the small community. "It does have a nice view. I imagine at night it's even better."

"Coming in?" Clint said, and he started walking toward the front door.

"Yes, wait up."

Clint stopped, waited for her, and they both entered the inn. The inside surprised them both.

"Interesting, I guess this is supposed to resemble the inside of a ship," Frankie said, pointing to the wall. "There's even a life saver, and with the way things have been going, we may need one."

"Welcome to the Clipper. Do you have reservations?" A small man with white hair and a face that had been out in the sun too many years asked from behind a wooden counter.

"Yes," Clint said as walked to the counter.

Frankie went in the opposite direction and studied a picture of an old clipper ship that hung from the wall. A metal plate with an inscription and some narrative was tacked to the wall just below the painting.

Clint finished registering and seeing Frankie studying the picture, he sent a short text to Buzz. "Can you have a jogging suit sent here today for LV police officer Frankie White. Include anything else that Dolly thinks would be appropriate." He grinned to himself after he put the phone away. Buzz or Dolly would likely be cursing him for the task and lack of info he provided, but he knew they would come through for him. They always had.

He walked over to Frankie. "Is this the original clipper?"

"The owner's family comes from a long line of sailors. The grandfather skippered this ship."

"Don't think I'm brave enough to be a sailor."

Frankie looked at him quizzically, "For a man that was barely phased at being fired at in short range, I'm surprised a little water would scare you."

"A little water? I guess you've never been at sea in a raging storm."

"Have you?"

"No, but I've seen it on TV. That alone scares me," Clint said and grinned. "Come on, let's check out the room."

"The room? I don't know what you're thinking, but you'd better be careful."

"Don't worry. It's a two-room suite."

Disappointment fluttered into Frankie's mind before she chased it away like an annoying gnat. The emotion surprised her.

The suite took up half of the second floor facing Las Vegas.

"I think we have both these doors," Clint motioned to the door to his left and opened the door in front of him. Before he entered, he studied the hallway again seeing another door on their side of the hall a further down and three doors across the hall. "Make yourself at home. I need to move the car around the back before it draws too much attention."

"Your car is going to draw attention no matter where you put it. A dozen bullet holes and no back window, I hope you didn't have any plans to trade it in." Frankie said. She walked over to the large window that faced the city. "What do you think, about fifteen miles? Yet you can see it as clear as can be." She heard the door close behind her. For a moment, she wondered if he might not come back.

The main room had a pull-out couch, and the smaller bedroom had a king bed. The furniture was nice but not impressive. Then again, it was hard to compete with some of the classier hotels on the Strip. She had spent a few nights in some of those rooms, and while she might have been impressed with the furniture, the nights she would rather forget. Too much alcohol and foolish decisions had ruined the many opportunities she had wasted and now regretted. But that was years ago, and she had cleaned up her act.

She had seven good years with the police department under her belt. She enjoyed the job and the comradery and believed she could make it to retirement. However, the job did mess with her personal life, as little as it was. Now in her thirties, it seemed like most of the men who hit on her were married and in search of a one-night fling. The few that were single usually ended up not wanting a relationship with a cop or not liking the hours she kept.

She glanced in the bathroom and realized how much she needed a shower. She looked into the mirror and saw a face with a patchwork of small cuts and hair full of cement dust. A large spot of blood adorned her collar. "What the hell," she murmured.

She locked the bathroom door and started to pick the debris out of her hair. After about five seconds, she gave up on the effort and decided to take a shower.

CHAPTER 11

Clint backed the car into a parking spot behind the building next to a retaining wall and beside a large pickup. Someone would have to drive or walk all the way to this last spot to see the car. He needed to get the back window replaced as soon as possible and wondered if coming all the way out here would be a problem.

His phone buzzed in his pocket.

"Clint, this is Dolly, how are you doing?"

Dolly was the third individual who worked at Special Section whom Clint had personally met. He believed there were one or two more on Deer's staff, but he had never talked to them or seen them.

"Trying to keep a low profile, but I'm not doing a very good job at it."

"You never do. I'm calling because you're going to have a package arriving this afternoon. I had to get into Officer White's personnel file to guess the sizes. It's not much, but it should get her through the next day or two."

"Thanks."

"Buzz and Ms. Deer have been working like crazy ever since you sent them that photo. In fact, I'm supposed to tell you not to leave the area until they give you the okay."

"I thought I was on a vacation."

"Don't think so. I don't know more, but I imagine she'll call you later today."

"If I'm back on company time, I also need a new rear

window for my car. Can you have someone come out and replace it?"

"Piece of cake," she said. "I'll get right on it."

"Thanks. I owe you a steak dinner." He ended the call before she could respond. He knew Dolly would know exactly where his car was parked to pass along to the auto window repair company. They kept track of Jim's car and phone twenty-four hours a day, every day. Before leaving his car, he grabbed his gym bag out of his trunk. Rolled up in the bag were a pair of jeans and a few other items of clothing. He reloaded his Beretta, placed it in the gym bag, and took the gym bag with him back to the room.

Clint entered their rented suite and heard the shower running. He threw his gym bag onto the couch and ignored the voice in his head that suggested he join Frankie in the shower. "Good way to get shot again," he said to himself.

Clint picked up the hotel phone and asked the man at reception about lunch choices in the small town. He also told the man that he was expecting a package and to be sure to call him when it arrived. The shower water shut off.

"Everything okay?"

"Just fine. Why didn't you tell me I looked like a mess?"

Clint grinned. "I never thought that. I hope you didn't use up all the hot water."

The bathroom door opened a few inches and Frankie stuck her head out. "What hot water? You don't have an extra tee shirt or something I can wear? I have blood on my uniform blouse."

"I may have." Clint pulled a red tee shirt out of his gym bag and handed it to her.

She closed the bathroom door.

Clint checked out the rest of the suite. The furniture had a heavy, dark appearance that he imagined might have been popular a hundred years ago, but the room was clean, and the air conditioning kept the room cool.

Frankie came out of the bathroom wearing her uniform trousers and the red tee shirt. Clint immediately noticed that the tee shirt was a little tight across her breasts.

"Too tight?" she asked, noticing his eyes.

"No, you look fine."

"I guess that's a compliment."

"Your face cleaned up well. I can see where your face was cut, but it's not bleeding, and the dried blood is gone."

Frankie placed her uniform shirt over the back of a chair. "This isn't going to work. I need clothes, and I need a phone. I also need backup."

"What we need first is lunch."

"I'm not hungry. I need to report in and find out what's going on."

"Lunch first, and while we're eating, we can find out where we can get you a phone and the rest. Didn't Yates tell you to stick with me?"

"Yes, but --," Clint cut her off.

"And that was barely an hour ago. You don't want to have them thinking you can't operate on your own for more than an hour, do you? Give me a little more time."

Frankie shook her head, but said, "A few more hours, but if Yates doesn't go to bat for me at headquarters, this will go bad for me. You can't just shoot someone and leave the scene."

"We didn't have a choice."

"We didn't know if more of them were coming after us."

"Frankie, they put a tracker on my car. They did come after us, and we have no reason to believe more weren't on the way. They knew where we were, and we were sorely outgunned at both locations."

"I still need a phone."

"At lunch, we'll ask where we can get you one out here."

"I didn't see a restaurant when we drove up. For that matter, I didn't see a store."

"The clerk told me a place to go. We can walk."

"You need to get your car fixed, too."

Clint smiled and extended his hand, "Still friends?"

"Ha! I don't even know who you are," but she accepted his hand and shook it.

"I'll take a quick shower, and we'll go eat."

"No rush, like I said, I'm not hungry."

CHAPTER 12

Clint led Frankie to a small building that looked like it might have been a house at some point. A small sign on the front window identified the place as the Clipper Café.

"A family operation?" Frankie asked.

"Apparently. The man at reception seemed to be very partial to this place."

"We'll see."

The café looked clean and pleasant and to Clint's surprise had all three of its visible tables occupied.

"Mr. Rogers?" a young teenage boy, wearing a white shirt and tie, approached them. He had a menu in his hand.

"Yes."

"I have your table in our Captain's room," he said, leading them into an adjacent room. One table, large enough to sit eight comfortably, sat in front of a large window that overlooked the valley leading to Las Vegas. The table was set for two and already had glasses of ice water. "Your server will be with you in one minute."

"Impressive kid," Clint said.

"Reservations? Mr. Rogers? I'm starting to feel like I'm in some strange movie. How did that all get arranged?"

"Like I told you, the reception guy at the hotel almost insisted we try this place, and I signed in as Mr. and Mrs. Rogers, so whoever is now looking for a guy named Smith won't know we're here. I thought you did that kind of stuff in witness protection."

"We do, but the witness isn't usually two steps ahead of us."

"This meal is also my treat. It may be our last, so don't order a salad."

"Don't worry, if you're buying, I'll splurge. You owe me," she said.

They both ordered the prime rib with mashed potatoes and the vegetable of the day. Clint also ordered a bottle of merlot for the two of them. There was no wine list and as the server was not sure what kind of wine they had, Clint simply asked her to bring them a merlot if the café had a bottle.

"Drinking on duty? You really must want to get me fired."

"You can't be expected to be on duty twenty-fours a day. There are no reinforcements coming, and I am going to try to get some sleep after I get back to the hotel."

Frankie looked at him and raised her eyebrows.

"I have a sneaky suspicion we may have a busy night, or at least I will."

"What are you talking about?"

"I don't know right now, but I think it has something to do with the Chinese guy."

"You mean Asian. Right now, we don't know if he's Chinese."

"True. Tell me a little more about yourself, Officer White."

"Not much to tell," Frankie said.

"Melanie said you were Hawaiian."

"I am. My mother is a native Hawaiian. My father is mixed, Black and Vietnamese. So that makes me mostly Hawaiian."

"Well, it's a beautiful mixture," Clint said and raised his water glass to toast her. He liked the way she smiled.

"I think I finally figured out what you do for a living. A used car salesman, right? How about your background? Are you a straight white American, maybe an Ivy Leaguer?"

"I've never done one of those ancestry things, but I believe somewhere in my past there is some Spanish blood. I was adopted, so I don't really know." Clint made a quick mental note that he had told her this. He kept his background stories to a small handful, but it still could get confusing.

"I saw from your tags that you're from Texas. What part?"

"I actually own property in a few different states, but for the most part I live in Texas, just outside of Harlingen. Is your family here in Las Vegas?

"No, they live in Honolulu. Sometimes I wish I did."

Their food arrived and their conversation became more intermittent. Frankie claimed to be a pretty good chef, having taken some classes from one of the better chefs in Las Vegas. Clint said he could grill a good hot dog, but that was about it. Neither had ever been engaged, and twice Frankie talked about how foolish she had been in her late teens and early twenties without elaborating. Clint didn't pursue the comments.

"That was good," Frankie said. She stretched her arms and stifled a yawn. "I may take you up on that nap. Separately, of course."

They agreed to walk around the small community in search of a phone store. The search turned into a casual stroll as they continued talking and getting to know each other. Frankie's comments about the town were correct in that their walk around the town only turned up a small gas station that carried a few essentials like beer, wine, and a wide assortment of salty and sugary snacks.

When they got back to their room, Clint suggested Frankie get some rest and went into the bedroom closing the door behind him.

Frankie sat down on the couch and stared at the closed door. She wanted to go into the bedroom, but kept telling herself how unprofessional it would be. Worse yet, what if he rejected her? Finally, she decided to use the room phone to call her office.

"Can you believe there were witnesses to both incidents today?" Frankie said to Clint an hour later. He had just come out of the bedroom.

"The one at the hotel for sure, but I didn't notice anyone at the second."

"I didn't either, but there were three men working in a building about a hundred yards down the street who watched the whole thing unfold from a second story window. They were able to corroborate what I had already told them."

"That's good," Clint said.

"It's better than good. The attack at the hotel was captured on security cameras, too. The vehicle at the second scene was the same vehicle caught on camera at the first."

"We knew that."

"You don't get my point. The press, nobody wants to believe the cops anymore. Without that footage and those witnesses, a month from now the story would be so twisted out there, someone would be suing the department, and I would be up on charges."

Clint understood her. A handful of bad cops had really hurt the reputation of the larger force. The police have over a million interactions with the public every day, yet it only takes one or two of them to paint the wrong picture of the entire service. Perfection is a good goal, but it's a faulty standard.

"More importantly, what's your status?" he asked.

"Yes, that did surprise me, too. My boss told me to stay with you for another twenty-four hours."

"Then what?" Clint asked.

"I don't know. I haven't been through something like this before. He did tell me this has the governor's attention and is already on the national news. The mayor is having fits and everyone has been called back in to work. Oh yeah, they can't spare a backup for me."

"I wouldn't want one."

She grinned, and the hotel room phone rang.

"Your boss?" Clint asked.

Frankie answered the phone. "Hello......yes......for us......okay, we'll be right down."

"Not your boss."

"No, the desk has a package for us. Did you order something?"

"Yes, earlier, let's go get it. It's for you." Clint walked out of the room, and Frankie followed him.

"You know, I'm supposed to be going out first to make sure it's safe. At some point, we need to start following procedure."

At the front desk, Clint retrieved the package and handed it to Frankie as they headed back to the room.

"It's for you," he said again.

"What did you do? You know it's against department regs for me to accept gifts like this."

"It's not from me, and when you don't need them anymore you can throw them away."

Back in the room, Frankie opened the package and laid out the contents on the couch. She looked at the sizes of the lightweight jogging suit and running shoes. "How did you know what size I wore?"

"I have a very discerning eye."

"Whatever that means," she picked up the pajamas. "Are these for me? They look like men's pajamas, long pants, long sleeves, and they button up to the neck."

"Not what I would've ordered for you," Clint said.

She smiled, "I like them."

CHAPTER 13

Theresa Deer sat at her desk in the bowels of the Marshal Service headquarters and studied her computer screen. Buzz sat opposite her, drumming his fingers on his right knee.

"This can't be a coincidence," he said.

Deer nodded. "This facial recognition software is damn good, but with billions of Chinese men out there, he might just be a good look alike."

"Running with a Las Vegas gang, operating an AR, and associated with what now appears to be an interesting land purchase adjacent to Nellis Air Force Base. One of the others now identified as being involved in the land purchase flew in from China just six weeks ago. We know nothing about him. Can't find a trace that he even exists."

"This second man?"

"Yes, ma'am. The one that is still living. And it is all related to the land now being acquired by a shell company."

"And Clint got himself in the middle of all this crap unwittingly, right?"

"Yes," Buzz knew she knew all this.

"So how do we extricate ourselves and get what we believe we know to the FBI and the military? Furthermore, how do we do it without flagging Clint's involvement to the world?"

"That may be near impossible, but I found something else out that may give us a way. This American shell company has recently purchased land near Cheyenne Mountain in Colorado and not that far from Peterson AFB."

"That's not good. Anywhere else?"

"Not that I've discovered, but I'm doing a deep dive into the finances of the company and then trying to identify a trail from the source to other companies involved in land deals in the U.S.," Buzz said. "May take a while though."

"This would all be routine, if it wasn't for Clint's involvement. We could just pass this on to the community, pointing out the Chinese connection. What we have to do now is get another agency or two to come up with the link on their own and get it out. Once it's anywhere in the system, we can grab it and expand on it without identifying ourselves as the original source."

"I think we can do that."

"We need to get it done tonight. The longer Clint is hung out there the longer he will be a liability to us. You know, my friend at CIA is hell bent on figuring out what we are really all about. He's still sniffing around the Ferma matter."

"He's a pest."

Deer nodded and said, "I don't believe he has any idea Clint took Ferma out or that we had anything to do with it, but the op does fit a pattern we've left behind. We need to shut down ops for a while and change how we do things. I think we've unwittingly left a pattern."

"Of untraceable hits."

"Exactly, that's what has him so interested. Dozens of high-level targets taken out over the last decade with no one taking credit, and no one knowing who's behind it all."

"You would think he wouldn't have time to be doing this."

"He's obsessed."

Buzz left her office and sat down at his desk to formulate

the plan. It should be easy to get the message out, but having another agency act on it was always a toss-up.

"Hey, Dolly, if we want to get the word out quick and taken seriously, but without leaving a trail back to us or Clint, what would be your game plan?"

"You're better at this than I am, Buzz, but I would use the old anonymous source strategy and contact the air base, the local FBI, and maybe a senator from Nevada. Of course, we would have to see if either senator would even care."

"I don't think going to a politician would be a good idea, but I agree with the air force and the FBI. My third choice would be some office in the Pentagon that deals with security policy. We can route an email through enough foreign servers that no one will be able to trace us and still have it look like it was sent from someplace in the Las Vegas area."

"That would work for the FBI and the base, but how and why would some local out there know about and contact some office in the Pentagon?" Dolly said.

"No, I'm with you there. We would have to give that office the information in a different way. Maybe I can locate an office in Taiwan that has an association of some sort with the one at the Pentagon and send an anonymous email that would appear to come from Taiwan, but with no specific person or office identified as the sender. The Pentagon may just think it's a tip from an ally that wants to stay anonymous."

"They'd have to reference the dead Chinese guy in Las Vegas and the land deal to get the Pentagon's interest."

"I think I can make that happen easy enough," Buzz said with a grin.

An hour later, he briefed Deer. She gave him the go-ahead,

and the messages went out. They had used this process to feed information to other U.S. and foreign agencies many times before. The people who worked for Deer had impressed her time after time, but it was the technology that she had at her fingertips that kept her amazed.

The computers and servers were top of or close to the top of the line, but no different than other government agencies that had some pull. What made her capabilities special were the artificial intelligence and advanced analytical software that were incorporated into the computers. That along with the covert, extraordinary access Special Section had to other agencies data made her office unique. She sometimes wondered if it was this access to information that made the need to keep the knowledge of her office's true purpose secret from virtually everyone, more so than a few foreign assassinations each year.

Sadly, a few of the nation's most important and powerful intelligence and security agencies had too often kept secrets from each other. After a national crisis, like nine-eleven, leadership would wring their hands and everyone would agree to do a better job of sharing, but a year later, everyone reverted back to their old form.

In fact, at the time, this unlimited access was the second layer of cover for the operational aspect of Deer's team. Nine-eleven did provide the need to create an office that could have community wide access and would facilitate the sharing of threat data. Not everyone bought into the idea, but a compromise was made when Special Section's size was cut to a point that made it seem impractical to be effective. At the time, only a few dozen principals in the intelligence community were made aware of this intelligence sharing role with the stand-up of Special Section. Back then, the emotions over nine-eleven prevented any of the agencies from saying no to the sharing of their data.

What these other agencies didn't fully comprehend was that once the office had the access, it was only a matter of time before the advanced software and artificial intelligence gave it the ability to siphon through the terabytes of data every day, culling out what was of interest to Deer and her team. Deer believed only a few now remembered this aspect of Section's mission.

Fortunately, Deer's office also had a confidential role that gave it legitimacy and was shielded by only a minimum amount of classification. Her office regularly produced multi-disciplinary counterintelligence reports for the Marshall service and shared with others who wanted it. This role would have given her office a logical reason to do its own reporting on the Chinese connection to the land deal; however, it could also link Clint to the office. A big leap, but enough to worry Deer.

Thinking of Clint, Deer called him.

"Clint, you've stumbled into an interesting situation. It appears the Chinese are buying up land next to a couple of our military bases."

"That's not good."

"No, it's not. They are doing it through an American company that seems to exist only on paper. It appears one of the land deeds you found had been requested to settle a land dispute a long time ago. The deed never got there, and as I imagine how more than one dispute was settled in those days, three existing family members were murdered one night. An investigation didn't find the killers, and the land went to the Jericho family by default. Relatives of the murdered family put up a protest, but they were all back east and never went out to Nevada to fight it."

"You're talking about stuff that is over a hundred years old, right?"

"That's right, but the deed makes it clear that the Whittens clearly owned the land. The challenge to the title is still in the system, if you can believe it, but would normally be ignored."

"After all this time, that old deed surely wouldn't affect the sale today," Clint said.

"Who knows, but it might make someone look deeper into the proposed sale. It makes no sense to kill anyone over it, unless you're the Chinese and have a lot riding on it."

"Especially, if they think uncovering their connection to the sale might cause further scrutiny of the company."

"Bingo. We've tied them to a recent land purchase near another installation. We're digging deeper," Deer said.

"What can I do?"

"Right now, just stay there. We're dropping hints at a few places, and hopefully someone else will be picking up this ball."

"Okay."

"Is the police woman still with you?"

"Yes, she's a big reason in my still being alive."

"You need to impress upon her the importance of keeping you out of this. You can tell her what we know, just let her know it's classified and is being passed on to the FBI and the military as we speak. Do what you can to make her understand the importance of keeping your name out of all this. Tell her we have a non-disclosure agreement coming for her to sign. They're mostly worthless, but they usually work on trustworthy people."

"Will do."

"We may have a simple task for you to do tonight."

"Okay, just call," Clint said.

CHAPTER 14

"Who was that?" Frankie asked. She had heard most of his end of the call. She had remained on the couch while Clint went into the bedroom for the call, but he hadn't closed the door.

"My boss. You'd like her."

"Your boss. So, you do have a life. What do you really do, Mr. Spyman?"

"Not really a spy, but my connection with the government is classified. She gave me permission to let you in on what they believe is going on."

"About time." Frankie tried to sound serious.

"Nothing I have said to you to this point was a lie or misleading. What I'm telling you now is information I just learned, too. This same information will be provided to the FBI and the military. You'll have to sign a non-disclosure agreement, but that's really just a formality. I trust you."

"We almost got killed together, twice, so I guess that warrants some trust both ways."

"One of the deeds I discovered, I don't know which one, had information identifying the legal owner of a section of land near what is Nellis AFB today. Apparently, this land or a section of land was in dispute way back then, and despite the years gone by, could throw a monkey wrench into the proposed sale of the same land today."

"How could it? That was over a hundred years ago."

"I don't know if it could, but the company trying to buy the land today is a front company for the Chinese, and they apparently don't want anyone looking too deeply into the purchase."

"I would think shooting up half of Las Vegas wouldn't be the way to maintain secrecy."

"You wouldn't think so, but I guess they're hoping they can get their hands on all copies of the deed and destroy them before it becomes public knowledge," Clint said.

"Forthsyte must have contacted the company or the seller. If he did, that may have been what started all this killing, but I still don't understand why anyone would want to kill anyone over some land."

Clint thought for a second. "Quietly walking away from the deal would've been the smart thing to do."

Frankie nodded her head first and then shook it. "Why didn't they?"

"A mistake. After Forthsyte and Melanie were killed, I sent a photo of both deeds to my boss. She's the one who discovered the Chinese connection and the background on the company. The same company had already purchased some property next to a military installation in Colorado."

"What? They are trying to spy on us, the bastards."

"Frankie, we are always trying to spy on each other. This must be part of a big operation, bigger than just the two land purchases."

"Why were the Demons involved in this? That's a local gang. What connection would they have with the Chinese?"

"I don't know, but they were and are connected. The Chinese man at the second attack was a Chinese government operative."

"How do you know that?"

"I sent his picture back to my boss. She identified him."

Frankie stared at Clint for a few seconds. "This is like some TV show or some spy movie. Things don't happen this fast. Are you playing me?"

"No."

"I need to call this in," Frankie said.

"No. Not yet. Like I said, my boss is passing the information along to other federal agencies. We'll make sure the police know. But if you tell them, the logical response from them would be to ask how you know this. I can't be linked any more than I already am. I'm sorry that I can't explain more at this time."

"I have to do something."

"Call them and ask them what the Chinese guy was doing supporting the gang in a shootout. That should help point them in the right direction," Clint said.

"Maybe I'll just wait until they call me."

"Okay, want to go for a walk?" Clint asked.

"A walk? Where?"

"Nowhere special. I feel like walking. Want to come?"

"Hey, I'm supposed to be in charge here. Remember I'm protecting you."

"And you're doing a great job, so don't let me walk alone."

Frankie grinned. "Okay, but let me put on that jogging suit and shoes."

They walked along a trail that led out of the small community along the side of the mountain. The terrain on both sides of the trail remained flat for several yards, and the trail meandered around most changes of elevation that tried to creep in too close.

The two eventually found a place to sit on a large flat rock and spent an hour talking about a variety of unimportant things to include how life must have been like back during the end of the nineteenth century.

When they returned to the room, they both noticed the hotel phone blinking.

"You must have received your call," Clint said, sitting down on the couch.

Frankie listened to the message and then without saying anything to Clint, punched a number into the phone. She talked briefly to someone she referred to as Mack, at one point asking him if they had identified the Asian shooter or had come up with a theory as to why he was involved. The call only lasted a minute.

"They have no idea why the guy was there with the Demons, but they are working it. So, that's good. We're pulling in all the members of the gang. Maybe by tonight they'll know more. They still want me to stay with you, but they want me to get you to tell me everything you haven't already told us."

"I've told you everything I know," Clint said.

She sat down close to him. "I may have to get rough," she said, trying to keep a serious look on her face, but her eyes gave her away.

"How rough?" Clint asked and leaned slightly to kiss her.

She kissed him and put a hand behind his head, kissing him again with more passion. Clint stood, picking her up.

"To the interrogation room," he said and carried her into the bedroom.

CHAPTER 15

The room had become dark when Clint's phone vibrated and danced on the small bedstand. He got up and took the phone out to the other room.

Frankie watched him walk and liked what she could see. She could hear him talk, but had no interest in eavesdropping. She had fallen for this man, but knew she needed to steer the relationship back to a more professional one. Sleeping with the person you're supposed to be protecting was a major no-no. Despite knowing this broke all the rules, Frankie looked at Clint and hoped he would get back in bed with her. He looked good standing there, straight, tall, in great shape, and naked.

"We need to take a ride and check something out," Clint said when he returned to the room.

"Immediately?"

Clint smiled, "Well, not immediately."

Thirty minutes later, they drove off in Clint's car that now sported a new back window. Clint didn't say anything about it, and while Frankie wanted to, she didn't, but she did wonder how and who replaced it.

"So, tell me again why we are going out?"

"My boss wants me to see if we can get some license tag numbers."

"Why? I thought she was sharing the information with the FBI."

"You're right. My guess is she's hoping to identify some of the players before everyone scatters."

"If we're going to do more than just drive by and get a few tag numbers, I'll need to call this in."

"Frankie, that's all I was asked to do. Afterwards, let's get a steak dinner somewhere."

"A steak dinner? You must be one of those high rollers. My momma warned me about guys like you. By the way, where is this place?"

"Don't know for sure, but it's in the nav system."

The nav system had been quiet, but Frankie saw that the screen did display directions for Clint to follow. She knew he didn't make any inputs into the nav system when they got into the car.

"I think I've gotten into something over my head. Just don't tell me magic is real or that you have superpowers. It's hard enough that things keep happening by themselves, like your once missing rear windshield. Are you going to press some button and make me forget everything when this is all over?"

"Like Men in Black, that movie?" Clint asked.

"Yes."

"No, although that would come in useful. It's just technology. My boss has the ability to remotely input a destination into my car, or for that matter, have a company come out and replace a rear windshield."

"Or get a gal some clothes. Makes sense, I guess," Frankie said. "Can they see what we're doing?" A look of worry crossed her face.

"No. You mean like us back in that room?" Clint asked and Frankie raised her eyebrows. "No, nothing like that."

"Good. So, is this boss of yours really your boss, or is she a personal valet? My boss wouldn't make any effort to get my stuff fixed or buy clothes for me."

"My boss doesn't exactly do those things. She has people working for her that do those things."

"Almost sounds like they pamper you. Wish I could find a job like that. Got any openings?"

"It's not a job one applies for, but I'll pass along your name."

"Does it involve travel?"

"Some," Clint said.

"I need to travel, see the world."

"Have you done any traveling?" Clint asked, not wanting to talk about his job any more. He knew the less she knew the better.

They talked about the few places she had been to and a few that Clint had been to while in the military. When they neared their destination, they became quiet.

"There," Clint said, looking at a small, dark building. He drove by without changing his speed and took the next right, stopping when the car was out of view of the building. "The building with the sign that said Carlson Development. Let's take an innocent stroll by it and see if we can get a few tag numbers."

"Might be hard in the dark. The small lot had no lights."

"All we can do is our best, then we get to go eat. Know any place around here?"

"There are a number of restaurants around here. This is mostly a business district, and it looks like Carlson Development has one of the few stand-alone buildings," Frankie said.

"We'll do the block. Seems like a deserted area for a city that never sleeps."

"Like I said, it's mostly professional businesses out here. Dentists, lawyers, realtors, banks, you know. People come to work during the day but don't return at night."

"Well, stay close. I may need some protecting." He reached out and took her hand. She let him.

They rounded the corner and started to cross the street when they saw a sedan turn into the parking lot for Carlson Development. It parked, and a man climbed out of the car. He stood still for a minute like he was scrutinizing the building and the area around it. Two men appeared from the shadows and walked up to him.

Clint and Frankie continued across the street and down the sidewalk. At first, they couldn't hear what the men were saying, but as they neared the front of the building the voices became louder.

"I said what are you doing here?" one of the men who had approached the driver demanded.

"I thought this was the address for a jewelry store. I'm just trying to figure out where I am," the driver said.

"That's bullshit," the man said and shoved the driver.

A smart man would have said something like he was sorry and climbed back into his car to drive away, but the driver did what too many men would do and let his pride get involved. He shoved the man back. Both men reacted by jumping the driver.

"Hey!" Frankie shouted and started running toward the fight.

"Damn," Clint said and followed Frankie. He could see that the driver knew how to defend himself, but something glistened in the dark reflecting a distant street lamp and slashed at the driver. He went down just as Frankie arrived.

"Police! Drop the knife," Frankie shouted. She had her police issued pistol in her hand.

The two men froze, and Frankie stopped a few feet from them. Clint stopped next to her and squatted next to the man on the ground.

"You drop your weapon," a strongly accented voice said.

"I'm a police officer, you don't want to do this," Frankie said. She didn't turn to face the man or do anything threatening.

"Drop it," the man said again, "or die now."

For the second time in as many days, Clint cursed himself for leaving his weapon in the car. He looked at the man with the gun. He looked to be in his forties, white, and deadly serious. The other two men resembled the gang members they had encountered earlier in the day.

"This guy is dying. We need to call an ambulance." Clint knew it was a dumb thing to say at this point, but he wanted to look like someone who hadn't recognized the dangerous situation into which they had gotten themselves.

One of the two men who assaulted the man on the ground next to Clint, reached out and grabbed Frankie's pistol. She hesitated but released it.

"Let's get them all inside," said the third man who seemed to be in charge.

"How are we supposed to get him inside," one of the gang members said, pointing to the man they had stabbed.

"You," the man in charge pointed the gun at Clint, "you carry him inside."

Frankie looked over at Clint. He could tell she was both terrified and angry. Clint lifted the bleeding man.

"This way and hurry up," the man with the gun stepped aside, motioning with his other hand for everyone to go by him.

Once inside, they all went into a small conference room with no windows. One of the gang members pulled out a chair and sat down. The other gang member leaned against the wall, holding Frankie's gun in his hand. "What now?" he asked.

Clint could see dozens of tattoos on the two Demon gang members. They both looked like they had Latin American roots. The one in the chair had a nasty scar across his chin. They wore jeans and dark tee shirts. In contrast, the middle-aged Caucasian man wore a tailored suit. His light brown hair cut close to his head.

"I need to make a phone call. You two really messed up." His accent made Clint wonder if he might be Cuban.

"What do you mean? Let's just kill them and dump them somewhere outside the city," the man with Frankie's gun said.

"We may have to, Rick, but she's a cop. They may know she was out here in the area. And who are you?" he asked Clint.

"Just her boyfriend. Look you can't kill us," Clint said, again trying to put some panic into his voice.

"Empty your pockets and put everything on the table. Now!"

"I think we should make them strip," Rick said.

"You two can help yourself to whatever you want," he indicated to the items now being put on the table. "But listen to me carefully, do not do anything else until after I make my call. We're more than likely going to catch hell for this already, so let's don't compound our problem anymore. No stripping, no killing, nothing until I get a chance to make my call. Understand?"

Both gang members nodded.

After their boss left, Frankie squatted next to the man on the floor. Clint leaned down close to her. "He's FBI," she whispered.

Clint nodded knowingly, and she gave him a curious look.

"Don't worry about him, you'll all be dead soon. And don't you worry, honey, we won't kill you right away."

"Hey, your phone is dead," the other gang member said to Clint while he looked through the items on the table.

"There's a trick to it," Clint said, standing back up. He took two steps toward the man with his phone, bringing him close to the man holding Frankie's gun.

"Get back there," he jabbed the gun at Clint. A fatal mistake that for a fraction of a second, the man wished he hadn't made.

Clint hit Rick's wrist hard, and with his other hand, he twisted the pistol out of Rick's hand. Without any hesitation he shot Rick between the eyes and then the second man in the heart. The two died before Frankie jumped up in surprise.

"Here," Clint tossed Frankie her pistol. She caught it. He leaned over the wounded FBI agent and removed a Glock semi-automatic from a holster the man was wearing. "Felt this when I carried him in. Figured he was FBI at the time."

"His name is Phil North. I've met him."

"Well, if we want him to live, we need to get him out of here. Can you carry him out?"

"Me?"

"No time to argue, I'll take care of the other guy." Clint didn't wait. He grabbed his wallet, keys, and phone from the table, and went to the door, cracking it open an inch. Gunfire erupted from somewhere outside the room, and rounds ripped holes through the door.

Frankie groaned, and Clint thought she might have been hit, but when he turned to look, he saw her pushing the large conference table over on its side to use as a barrier.

Clint used his foot to push the door open a few more inches. Again, shots rang out, and two more holes appeared in the door, and one round pushed through the drywall next to Clint.

Someone shouted from the back of the building, and Clint thought he heard a whooshing sound. Another two shots were fired into the room, once again making Clint duck down and move away from the door. After about fifteen seconds of silence, Clint smelled smoke, and when he looked at the crack between the door and the wall, he saw a few whisps of smoke sneaking into the room.

He looked back at Frankie. "I think they're burning this building down."

"That means they'll be leaving. That may give us time."

"How is he?"

"Too much bleeding, I don't think he'll make it," Frankie said.

"I'll make it," a weak voice said from behind the table.

"Phil, we'll get you out of here," Frankie said.

Another gunshot sent a round through the door, and the door opened a few inches more.

"They want to keep us trapped in here, so the fire can get us," Clint said.

"Where are we?" Phil asked in a weak voice.

"They made us all come inside. Clint carried you in. What were you doing here?" Frankie asked.

"Got an anonymous tip. After all the killing today, I thought

I'd drive by and just take a look. You know, see if the company really existed."

"You relax now."

"Did you call for backup?"

"I don't have my phone and his battery might be dead," Frankie said.

"Use mine," Phil said.

Clint heard the conversation while he took the occasional peek outside the room through the small opening of the door. His phone worked fine as did its safety measures since it didn't function in someone else's hand. Clint's fingerprints activated the phone. He had already considered calling 911, but hoped he and Frankie could get out of the building before everyone arrived.

Clint heard someone shout again from the back of the building. He thought it sounded like "we gotta go." He waited for about ten seconds and was about to push the door open when all hell broke loose. Someone turned a weapon to fully automatic and shredded the door and a good part of the drywall around it. Clint instinctively dove away from the door and onto the floor. As he did, he felt a number of stings to his right arm.

The building became somewhat quiet again. Clint could hear the crackling of the fire but no voices. He looked at his arm and saw several small cuts and a few pieces of wood and drywall sticking to his arm. A little blood oozed out of four spots where the cuts were deep enough to draw blood. Glancing back at the table, he asked "Are you both okay?"

"We're good," Frankie said. "I'm calling 911 right now."

Thick smoke started drifting into the room. Clint could see

that the smoke had also become a lot thicker outside the room, but he couldn't see any flames.

"We need to get out now. I think the shooters have left. They are likely hoping that last volley would keep us in here until we couldn't get out," Clint said. "Come on."

"Let me help you get up," Frankie said.

"I'll need it. I hit my head hard when I went down. I think that's why I blacked out."

Clint looked back at them and saw Frankie help Phil to his feet. He looked like he wouldn't stay upright for long. Frankie wrapped her left arm around him to support him. Clint saw she gripped her police issued Glock in in her right hand.

"Let's get outside and away from this fire. I'll lead the way and clear the area if necessary." He pushed the door open and looked out. Seeing nothing but smoke, he stepped out.

CHAPTER 16

The outer hallway and adjacent rooms were empty. Clint spotted dozens of spent cartridges on the floor inside the doorway to one of the rooms. Feeling sure their attackers had fled, Clint joined Frankie and helped her half carry Phil as he tried to walk. All three were coughing by the time they walked out into the fresh night air.

Clint could hear the sirens approaching them as they helped Phil sit down. They leaned him against the knee-high cement wall that lined part of the yard, and Clint put the agent's pistol back in its holster.

"Thanks, must have dropped it," Phil said in a weak voice.

"Frankie, listen to me," Clint said. He pulled her by the hand a few steps away from the FBI agent. "I can't be here when everyone arrives. Trust me, I'll come get you around six in the morning from your place. Take care of Phil and do whatever reporting you think is necessary. Tell them I went back into the building to get my wallet, or that I panicked and ran off after we got outside. It doesn't matter. Let them know that you believe I'll get back in touch with you, so they won't make finding me a priority. Anything, but I have to go. And you'll need to come up with some excuse as to why we were here." He kissed her on the lips and left before she could say anything.

He didn't go straight to the sidewalk and back to the car the way they came. He crossed the small parking lot, taking a quick photo of the tags on the two other cars in the lot before walking through the parking lot of the building next door. From there he stepped out, crossing the sidewalk and got into his car. The fire engines arrived before he pulled his Lincoln away from the curb, so he made a U-turn from his parking spot and drove away from all the excitement.

A half dozen blocks away, he found a café advertising their breakfasts and lunches on their street side windows. The lights were on, and Clint could see a few people moving around inside. He went inside and by doing so added thirty three percent to the café's customer crowd. Dinner must not be its specialty, he thought.

Feeling his phone vibrate, Clint removed it from his pocket and saw that someone at Section had responded to the two photos he had sent minutes before. The text read, "Received the tag numbers and will follow up. Realize things are hot there right now. Gave your car a new address to check out. Call when you get there, before you make any contact."

"Will do after I finish my pancakes and sausage," he replied, and then had a thought. "Can you find a cell number for FBI Agent Phil North, Las Vegas Field Office, and send to me?"

His phone vibrated again, this time with a phone call.

"What's going on, Clint?" Deer asked.

Clint thought she didn't sound too happy.

"When we went by the address you sent us this afternoon, everything went to hell. Frankie and I were walking in front of it when two men jumped Agent North in the building's small parking lot. They stabbed him, Frankie's training went in, and she tried to rescue him. I guess she did, but in the process, we were escorted into the building by three armed men. North was unconscious at the time. Once inside, we managed to escape before the building burned down around us."

"Why do you want North's phone number? You don't need to worry about him or strike up a new friendship."

"I don't believe he has his phone at the moment. He gave it to Frankie to use. I'm hoping she still has it, so I can reassure her I'm safe and prevent her from overreacting to my leaving the scene. She couldn't leave. North may not make it, and she had to stay until the medics arrived."

"I'm glad you left the scene, and I've got half a mind to send you to Alaska right now to hide in the bush somewhere for a month or two. However, we need to extricate you from this situation in a way that ends any interest in you. Additionally, I would still like you to check out the address we sent to your car. This thing has become big, real big here in DC and obviously there."

"I may take you up on that Alaska trip."

"You may not have a choice." The phone went silent, and Clint realized she had ended the call.

Clint was paying his bill when a text arrived providing him with North's phone number. He thought by now North had reached the hospital, and Frankie was still being grilled by both her LVPD superiors and the FBI. This would not be a good time to call. He wondered if she lied about why she happened to be in the area, or if she told them about him.

"What a mess you've gotten yourself into," he said to himself.

"Excuse me," the cashier, a young man with long blond hair and thick glasses, said.

"Just rambling to myself."

"Is that your car out there?"

Clint looked out the front window and acknowledged that it was his car.

"Are those bullet holes? You can barely see them from here, but I was by the window a minute ago and could see them. There must be a dozen of them."

"Yes, I was parked at the Orleans today and there was a drive by or something in the parking lot."

"I heard about that. Sounded like a gang war. A bad one at that."

"When I went out and saw what happened to my car, I told the hotel management I was going to sue them. I don't know if my insurance will cover it," Clint said.

"Good luck on that. My insurance company wouldn't even pay for new glasses when I broke my old ones. I guess it was just good that you weren't outside when it all went down."

"Indeed," Clint said and walked away.

The new navigation settings had him driving west out of Las Vegas to a suburb that consisted of twenty or so very expensive homes, each surrounded by at least an acre of land. The place reeked of wealth and exclusivity. A wide gate with a security guard blocked visitors' entry, and a large placard fastened to the six-foot, limestone rock wall identified the neighborhood as Sunset Luxury Villas.

Clint drove by the entrance and up a nearby rise that wouldn't qualify as being called a hill. He pulled off the road and climbed out of the car. A quarter moon gave off scant light, and the dark surroundings seemed lifeless. A light dusty breeze brought with it an odor Clint didn't recognize. Something small darted across the road about thirty yards away.

He looked down into the Sunset Luxury Villas subdivision

where most of the homes looked dark. He could make out a small vehicle moving slowly through the neighborhood, going up and down each street. Security, he thought.

Another call came in from Deer.

"What do you see?"

"It's a nice neighborhood, gated with security at the gate and someone driving around inside. Looks like a rock wall goes all the way around it."

"I was afraid of that. Let's not try anything tonight. The FBI will be working this for sure now that one of their own has been assaulted. I need you to get any of your stuff out of your room at the Orleans and the one at the Clipper. Don't check out; we'll take care of it, and we'll get you into a different place to stay hidden for tonight."

"Only Frankie knows about the Clipper."

"Yes, but you have more faith in her than I do. Keep your head down."

Clint's frustration on the drive back into Las Vegas didn't last long. He caused all this by digging up his buried treasure. Deer wasn't to blame, as none of this fit into his normal role with Special Section. Even if Section had discovered the information about the Chinese buying up land next to a couple of military bases through its own analysis, it would have shared that information, but no hunters would be sent out to look into it. This simply wasn't something in which Section would normally get involved. No, Clint caused this mess, and if Deer had somehow compounded it, it was by sending him out to take a photo of a couple of license tags. Something she now likely regretted.

Removing the few items from his room at the Orleans Hotel

and then at the Clipper took minutes. The drive to both and back to the new place, however, took over an hour. He called Frankie early in his drive. She still had the FBI agent's phone.

"I forgot I still had this," she said after Clint identified himself. "Where are you?"

"Calling from my car. How's Phil?"

"Better than we thought earlier, but he lost a lot of blood, and the bump on his head when he fell caused a concussion. Am I going to see you again?"

"If I disappear now, how much of a stink will that cause?"

"More than you probably want. Hold on," Clint felt like she was walking away from anyone she was around, and when she spoke again, her voice was almost a whisper. "I'll help you disappear, but I need some help in wrapping up our involvement in this mess."

"See you in the morning?"

"Yes." She gave him the location to a Starbucks near the Flamingo Hotel, and they agreed to meet at seven thirty.

Clint made one more stop before arriving at the motel where Section had reserved a room for him and traded out the car's license tags for a set from Pennsylvania. He also swapped the registration and insurance paperwork, along with his own driver's license for one under the name of Bud Foster.

When he saw the hotel, he was glad Frankie wasn't with him. He doubted she would stay here. The place looked like it rented rooms by the hour. Obviously, Section was punishing him.

CHAPTER 17

He arrived at the Starbucks at seven but walked by it and found an indoor seat at a nearby pastry café that gave him a good view of both the wide pedestrian walkway and Starbucks. He trusted Frankie, but also knew she had to be under a great deal of stress.

She showed up at seven thirty-five, and after looking around for a minute, she ordered a drink and sat down at an outside table with her back to him. Clint waited four minutes, and not seeing anyone else who seemed to have any interest in her, he joined her.

"Late," she said. She looked tired, but still good, Clint thought.

"You look prettier than I remember."

"Lame. Where did you stay last night? I called the Clipper, but they said you had checked out."

"At a dive, I think I'm being punished."

For whatever reason, that made Frankie smile. "I told them you panicked last night and took off, but that you promised me that you would call me today. Both Phil and I vouched for you. With all the stuff going on, no one really cared that you weren't there."

"How's Phil?"

"Barring an infection, he'll be okay. I learned after I talked to you last night that he would've bled out in another ten minutes. We all got lucky last night."

"What can I sign or do so I can leave here today or

tomorrow?"

"Man, that was a short time romance, and I was thinking of introducing you to mom and dad."

"It's not you, it's me," Clint said, causing Frankie to laugh.

"You have that right, Clint. Can I talk you into coming down to the precinct? We could wrap this up down there."

"No, believe me that would just lead to more curiosity, more questions. Someone would become more interested in who I am rather than what has happened."

Frankie knew he was right. She routinely ran into other cops who wanted to further interrogate the witness she was assigned to protect. Someone always thought the witness was somehow part of the blame.

"So far, everyone is accepting the story as we've presented it to them," she said.

"Hopefully, because it's all true."

"It was up until last night. I lied to them and told them we were going out for dinner and just happened to be walking by the building."

"Well, that's mostly true. We were on our way to dinner with just a slight detour."

"Reminds me, I never got that dinner."

"Tonight, I guarantee it."

"Fortunately, Phil remembered being accosted by the two men, and that he was in the parking lot alone. His recall after that is blurry, but he does remember us helping him out of a burning building. They took his weapon and mine to do the usual tests. He doesn't remember if he shot anyone or not while he was in the building."

"I don't know if I hit anyone with his gun or not. The two I took out in the room were with yours."

"I know."

"If you haven't said anything about it yet, just tell the truth. Tell them I have a military background and just reacted the way I did."

"If I do, someone will insist on your getting interviewed at our place or the Bureau's. I don't see how we can avoid that."

"I'll come up with something," Clint said.

"May I join you two?"

Clint looked up. "Damn, Buzz, why didn't you give us a heads up?" He stood up to shake hands.

"What and spoil the surprise."

Frankie stood, too. "Excuse me, but someone needs to introduce us." She looked at Clint.

"Don't give me those dagger eyes. I didn't know he would show up like this, and I didn't tell him where or when we were meeting this morning."

Frankie looked at Buzz, her eyes challenging him. "Who did you follow? Him or me?"

"Neither, and forgive me if my arrival like this is a cause for concern. I assure you my presence this morning will be brief and cause you no harm, Frankie. If I may call you that."

Frankie looked at Clint. "He's one of you guys?"

"Yes and no," Buzz answered for him. "Clint is a field operative. I am a bean counter from our headquarters. Clint, would you mind leaving us alone for ten minutes, maybe take a walk up and down the Strip for some exercise."

"What if I say no?" Frankie asked.

"I'm here to answer some of your questions," Buzz said.

She hesitated but said, "All right, but you come back. You

don't want me to come looking for you."

Clint smiled, winked at her, and left.

"So, start talking," she said to Buzz.

Clint strolled out to the Strip and started walking. Things hadn't changed since the last time he was here, but he was still impressed with the size of the hotels. He timed his walk to give them fifteen minutes. When he returned, Frankie was sitting alone, and he could see Buzz in the distance walking away.

"Everything okay?" he asked Frankie.

"Yes. He told me all your secrets," she said with a grin.

"I don't have many."

"He had me sign that form."

"It's a formality. You know, national security and all."

"He still didn't tell me exactly what you do. I asked, but he wouldn't say. What is it, one of those 'if I tell you, I'd have to kill you' things?"

"Not that exciting," Clint said. "It's just what I do that is secret."

"He said that and that what you did, you did in a way so it, whatever it is, could not be connected to the United States."

"Hence, our dilemma."

"I can deal with it."

"Thanks. Regarding this mess I got you into, tell me what I can say or do to make your life a little easier?"

"I want to record an interview of you to document everything that has happened from when we walked out of the Orleans yesterday through our escape last night. I'll need it to be thorough, and at this point it's really just necessary to corroborate what I'm telling everyone."

"You want to do it here?"

"No, I have reserved us a room here in the Flamingo. I didn't think you'd come back to the station, so I got the room. That way if I get a little rough with you, no one will hear your cries for help," she said, grabbing his hand and leading him into the hotel.

"Do I need my lawyer?" Clint asked and smiled.

CHAPTER 18

By early afternoon, Clint could no longer see any remnant of Las Vegas in his rearview mirror. He had made one stop leaving the city to deposit the two checks, but since then it had been non-stop. He put the car's cruise control at seventy-three and an old Sade CD in the car's player. This had been the second time in three years he had been to Las Vegas and had yet been able to play the tourist. Maybe he would have to give up on the city.

Clint traveled north and wondered how far he could drive before he ran out of roads. It would take a few hours to get out of Nevada, and he had traveled a similar route a few years earlier. That time he was following someone. This time he could go wherever, and he figured that's just what he would do. He took state highway ninety-five through Tonopah and then over toward Carson City where the state road merged into I-80. Further north, he stayed with the state road as it went into Oregon and started looking for a place to spend the night.

No one from Special Section had tried to contact him since he had seen Buzz that morning, and that was fine. Clint figured he really did need to disappear for a few weeks if he wanted to keep his job, and the job had grown on him. Thinking about it made him feel a little strange. How could it be normal to feel a contentment at being an assassin. Section could use the label hunter, and it fit, too, but boil it down, and he was a government assassin.

He rationalized it many times by telling himself the threats he "neutralized" were indeed threats to national security. If he hadn't been successful in what he did, many innocent Americans would have died. Just keep telling that to yourself, he thought. Besides, what else could he do. His first and only other job was in the military where he excelled in combat in Southwest Asia.

Even now, driving a car with a dozen bullet holes in it, didn't make him feel uncomfortable. Oh well, he thought, get over it, because you are what you are.

He half expected when he reached the Oregon border, he might see more signs of civilization, but he found this part of Oregon as sparsely populated as Nevada. The MKZ was on fumes when he finally found a gas station and a motel near a place called Burns Corner. He would have to register as Bud Foster, remembering he needed to swap out the plates on the car and become himself again, but he would do that in the morning.

Muskie's Tavern's neon lights did a better job of lighting up the motel's parking lot than the motel's own lights. In fact, the motel's lot seemed to be the overflow parking lot for the tavern as well. Clint wondered if the hotel's customers were mostly the late-night customers of the tavern trying to find romance or perhaps a few hours escape. He considered getting back in his car and leaving without checking in, but an old man in overhauls greeted him from the motel's front porch.

"This is the best and one of the few motels for miles around here. Don't let the tavern scare you off. Besides, I could use the business."

"Can you fix me up with a room away from the tavern in case it gets noisy?" Clint asked.

"Sure, my name's Chester," he stretched out a hand.

"Hello Chester, I'm Bud." He noticed the man had an old ball cap that identified him as a Viet Nam War vet. "When were you in the war?"

Chester grinned. "You know, war was never declared. Not that it mattered much to us when we were being shot at. Come on in." Chester opened the door for him.

Clint entered the hotel and looked around. The lobby looked clean enough.

"I was over there in sixty-nine. Better than sixty-eight, I've been told, but then, I was scared enough in sixty-nine."

"Can't help but be scared. I was in Southwest Asia a few years back. I know the feeling."

"Yeah, I don't think it matters where you are. Got out of the army as fast as I could after I returned. Looking back, I wished I'd stayed in. I just drifted around and wasted a good dozen years before I finally settled down."

"This where you're from?" Clint asked.

"Not really, but I've been here for the last ten years and will probably die here. It's nice country."

Clint paid cash for the room, and perhaps because he paid in cash, he didn't have to register. The tax man would never know, he thought and grinned. "Chester, is the food next door any good?"

"Actually, it's quite good. The crowd there now is for dinner, later a different crowd will show up for the dancing, and then the hardcore will show up. Unless there's a fight or two, the police usually stay away, and it doesn't get too noisy. They usually ignore the prostitutes that show up around midnight."

Chester thanked him and left in search of his room. He

wondered why Chester made the comment about the prostitutes. Maybe to warn him or maybe to let him know he didn't have to drive around looking for them, if he was so inclined. He wasn't.

Buzz called him while he was walking to Muskie's.

"What's up?" Clint asked.

"Nothing, just wanted to let you know that despite a lot of effort by the police and the feds, nothing has happened in Vegas after you left. Everyone has vanished. Even the gang members have scattered. The few that have been rounded up say they know nothing, and it's possibly true."

"Much hysteria about my leaving?"

"No. You're a complication for them. Pretty much everyone who you could testify against is dead. Between the FBI's security concerns and the publicity concerns by the PD and city, I think they want to circle their wagons and control what the press gets told. Better for everyone, and if you stay disappeared, so much the better."

"Guess that makes sense," Clint said.

"In case you're interested, the FBI agent should be released from the hospital tomorrow."

"Good."

"And as far as we can tell, that pretty lady you were with today has been put on administrative duties, but I don't think is in any real trouble."

"That's good, too. Everyone up there okay with the way things have turned out."

"So far. A lot of strange stuff in the Chinese message traffic but nothing that makes any sense to anyone. Oh yeah, the company's branch office in Colorado Springs closed, and everyone disappeared from there, too."

Clint knew he was talking about the same shell company that had been trying to purchase the land next to Nellis AFB by Las Vegas.

"That's good."

"Yes. My guess is the FBI will find a way to get into that place as quickly as they can."

"Makes sense. Hey, Buzz, I'm thinking about driving up to Dawson Creek in Canada. Seems to be about as far north as I'll go. Would you mind seeing if there's a body shop, a private one, that can patch the bullet holes in my car. I have a few."

"Piece of cake. I'll text you what I find. By the way, isn't that a new car?" Clint heard him chuckle as he ended the call.

Later, as he climbed into bed, he remembered the dinner he had promised Frankie and wondered if he would get another chance.

CHAPTER 19

Frankie sat at a small table at Bev's Bagel and Buns Bakery in downtown Las Vegas. She had the day off and thought she would go to the gym after her meeting with Agent North. She had put on her black and white exercise outfit, figuring her meeting with the FBI agent was more social than work related. He had called her the night before and wanted to meet this morning. Like Frankie, he had been told to take a few days off, too.

She knew the feds, the state, the county, and the police department had gone into overdrive trying to round up everyone involved in the murders, the assault on a federal officer, and some security matter that was only discussed at the highest levels behind closed doors. She smiled with the self-satisfaction of knowing what the whispers were about. The fact that she couldn't let anyone know didn't bother her. It helped keep her memory of Clint alive, and she liked that.

Her boss had told her that losing Clint might hurt her performance record in the future. She argued that after being shot at on three occasions and then almost burned alive, how could anyone blame him?

"Well, fortunately for us with all this other stuff going on, his disappearance will soon be forgotten. After all, he could be dead by now," her boss had said.

"Not a comforting thought," she said, but she knew the truth.

She chewed on her blueberry bagel and waited. North had

wanted the nine o'clock meeting time, so he could sleep a little longer than usual. She imagined the knife wound had knocked a lot of his strength out of him. Ten minutes late, he walked into the bakery dressed in shorts, sandals, and a large comfortable looking Hawaiian shirt.

"Sorry," he said and went to the counter, returning with a large cup of coffee, a chocolate chip bagel, and three packs of cream cheese. "The pain meds knock me out. I tried to take a lower dose last night, and I woke up after midnight in a lot of pain. I took some more, and the stuff knocked me out until a little while ago."

"How is the injury?"

"Only painful when I move. I roll around a lot at night, so that doesn't help. I have my full range of motion and everything should be back to normal soon. I don't remember much of my first night at the hospital."

"That's understandable."

"Still, I don't like not remembering stuff. That's one reason I wanted to meet with you. Can you fill me in with what specifically happened? Please start from the beginning, from where you saw me being assaulted."

"You obviously remember some of it," Frankie said.

"Yes, and I remember what people told me happened, but you two were there."

"By accident, we were going out for dinner, and I got the address wrong in my head. We were just about to turn around and head back to the car when I saw one of the guys push you. Actually, you three were shouting at each other which caught my attention first."

"I remember all that. My mind kind of goes fuzzy after I fell."

"You hit your head."

North nodded. "I know that much, and Jack, a guy I work with has given me a brief version of what happened after that. However, I need to know more, so please."

"Sure, but I need to get a refill; this may take a while," Frankie said and walked over to pour herself a half of a cup from a coffee urn that sat on a side table near the cashier.

He listened without interrupting or even saying a word, making Frankie feel a little uncomfortable. She told him everything exactly how it happened. He had come to at some point around the time Clint had shot the two men in the room with them or shortly thereafter, and she didn't want to be caught in any lie.

"Thanks," he said when she finished. "I don't have any recall of being carried into the building by Clint, right? That's his name, Clint?"

"Yes."

"I remember the noise."

"What noise?" Frankie asked.

"The shooting, all the shooting, and the smell of smoke. I vaguely remember getting outside, because I can remember a sense of relief when the air cleared. I know I was put in an ambulance, but if I had to swear to anything about the ambulance crew, or the time, or which hospital they took me to, I couldn't do it. I mean I learned later which hospital, but at the time." He shook his head.

"You talked to me that night a little while we were still in that room."

"I believe you, but I can't recall any of it."

"Other than making you feel uncomfortable, I guess, it

doesn't matter. The two guys who attacked you are dead, and you never had a chance to look at the third man. If, somehow, we get this third man into court, your testimony would all be hearsay anyway."

"Who is this guy, Clint? Sounds like he may have saved us all."

"He did. I don't know that much about him. He is former military, and he has quick reflexes. That's for sure, because when that thug stuck my gun in his face, he took it from him in a flick of the eye."

"And he shot both guys, right?" North asked.

"Yes. They were going to kill us. They said so. Like I said, the third guy, the one in charge had instructed them not to kill us until he had a chance to call someone. The two guys wanted to kill you and Clint right away. They planned on raping me first."

He thought about that for a second. "Even my strait-laced, 'give the bad guy every chance to turn himself in' way of thinking tells me Clint did the right thing, too. I wish I could thank him."

"I don't think he needs any thanks, he saved himself, too, you know."

"Still."

Frankie nodded.

"I hear he's gone."

"I think he got tired of being shot at."

"How was he involved in all this?"

"What do you mean?"

"Why was he getting shot at, and then why was he also at the same place I was?"

Frankie froze for a second. She had said too much. "His getting shot at is a long, long story, which I doubt has much to do with our night together. I'm the one that ran in to rescue you, Phil. He tried to hold me back, so I wouldn't get hurt."

North studied her but didn't say anything else.

"How long do they have you on medical leave?" she asked.

"I see the doctor next week. I think after that I'll be able to return on limited duty status. At least, I hope that's the case. How about you?"

"I imagine I'll be riding a desk for a while. It sucks, but it can't last forever. Probably put me out on traffic for the rest of my career."

He grinned. "Don't think that. Besides, we can always use new agents."

"Thanks, I may just take you up on that someday."

"Think we'll see Clint again?"

"I think so. He knows how to get in touch with me, and he said he would."

"If he does, I sure would like to thank him."

"I'll make sure you have a chance to. He's a good guy who has been through a lot here in our peaceful little city."

"Peaceful, ha! What part of this peaceful city do you live in?"

Frankie didn't believe he was really interested in where she lived. "Anything else? I don't mean to be rude, but I need to get to the gym."

"No, I thank you for your time. I'll walk you out." He grimaced as he stood up.

She started to reach over to help him, but he shook his head.

"I can do it," he said.

Once they were outside, they both turned to the right and started walking. A lady jogged by and then stopped about five yards in front of them. She groaned and bent over, grabbing her knee.

"Are you okay?" Frankie asked.

"Need any help?" Phil asked.

Bent over, she looked up at them, and something in her eyes didn't look right. Frankie stopped and heard a crack. She looked at Phil, seeing him fall to the ground just as the woman slammed into her and drove her toward a white cargo van at the curb. Frankie fought back but had no time, as someone in the van reached out and lifted her inside. The woman followed her in and hit her. She faded out of consciousness with her last vision being Agent North dropped next to her.

CHAPTER 20

Clint drove the small fishing boat up onto the shoreline of Lake Babine. He had been out on the large lake for a few hours and needed to get rid of some of the coffee he had been drinking. He looked all around and saw no one. In fact, except for a few other fishing boats he had not seen anyone all morning.

The fishing had been fair. He caught two large trout early on but nothing in the last ninety minutes. In fact, that ninety minutes had reminded him why he didn't fish very often. He did enjoy being out, though, and the peaceful surroundings were relaxing.

The manager at the lodge had offered to have his chef cook any fish Clint could catch and to pay him for any extras he may not want to keep. Clint didn't want the money, but he looked forward to the chef preparing the fish.

A rustle nearby in the woods caught his attention. He glanced in the direction of the sound and saw a moose peering at him. Clint remained still. He knew a moose would normally ignore him, but he also knew they could be quite dangerous if they got agitated.

He had once heard that moose killed more people in Alaska each year than bear. He wasn't in Alaska, but he didn't think that would matter much to the moose. If a bear didn't eat you, he would leave you cut up and bleeding, but you would still be mobile, and even if alone, you could take yourself somewhere for help. If a moose attacked, his hooves and antlers were more likely to break several bones leaving a person immobile. Without someone to help, a person usually died within fifty yards of the moose attack after days of agony.

In this case, the moose turned his head and disappeared. Clint walked back to his boat, started the engine, and steered the boat away from land. After a couple of minutes, he slowed the boat and dropped a fishing line with a shiny spinner into the water off to the side and behind the outboard engine. Keeping the speed of the boat slow, he began trolling. The sun climbed higher in the sky, and Clint finally decided he had enough nature for one day. He headed back to the lodge but kept the speed of the boat down and left the fishing line in the water.

In the large lake, it took over an hour to reach the lodge with no additional fish to justify the slow pace. He had caught two fair-sized fish, though, and thought that was sufficient to show he wasn't an abject failure as a fisherman.

"They look great," Rex, the manager, said a few minutes later when Clint showed him the fish. "We can make you a super dinner with these. Congratulations."

"Thanks, how big do the fish get out there?"

"They can get quite large, but this size is the best for catching and eating."

"You're not just blowing smoke? Are these really a good size?" Clint asked.

"These are perfect. Most people who fish here are very pleased with a catch this size. We do have our experts who have been fishing here their whole lives. They know where the deep holes are and know how to catch the bigger ones."

"How big?"

"Lake trout up to twelve kilos, that's over twenty-five pounds."

"Holy cow, that's huge."

"We have rainbow trout up to ten to twelve pounds."

"Why isn't it more crowded here?"

Rex grinned. "As you see, we are in the middle of nowhere. The lake is big, so more people can be out there without the lake feeling crowded. This is a workday, and perhaps the most important, there are millions of lakes around here. Many people have their favorite lake or stream."

"I'm from Texas where we don't have a million lakes or this many trees. It's really beautiful up here."

"Well, I wish I could take credit for that, but all I can do is offer you a fantastic dinner tonight. What time would you like it to be ready for you?"

"How about six thirty?"

"See you then."

Clint went to his room in the lodge glad that he hadn't been called by anyone in the last few days. The lodge didn't have many customers, but the restaurant did fair business as it appeared to be a favorite of the local population. He had eaten dinner in the restaurant after arriving the day before and was impressed.

The auto body shop in Dawson Creek that patched his car had not done a first-rate job, but they did everything in one day and had even talked him into letting them try to fix some of the shredded interior. The best that could be said now was that no one would recognize that the slightly off-color blotches of paint were hiding damage caused by gun shots. At the lodge, parked among several old beat-up vehicles, his Lincoln looked just fine.

Before dinner, Clint jogged for a couple miles on the narrow road that did little more than bring people to and from the lodge. He thought about the moose he saw earlier and wondered about the variety of local wildlife as he ran. Other than squirrels and birds, he didn't see any.

Dinner that night proved to be delicious. He ate his trout prepared in a variety of ways: pan fried and lightly crusted, boiled in a potato soup, and cooked in a creamy fish ragout. He even found small pieces of cooked trout in his salad.

"How was it?" Rex asked. He had been making his rounds talking to the restaurant patrons and stopped at Clint's table. He still wore the old jeans and red corduroy shirt that he had on earlier when Clint had talked to him.

"Excellent. I didn't know there were so many ways to prepare fish."

"Everything but the rolls had your fish in them," Rex said. "I told you our chef was good. He came here from Victoria to help with his mother. She lives in a cabin not far from here."

"Nice of him."

"Yes, she is still in pretty good shape, but her vision stinks, so she can't drive. He showed up looking for a job the day after he arrived in the area. I think his mom must have recommended us."

"Probably did," Clint said. "I didn't see many other restaurants around here."

"True. Anyway, it was a real blessing for us. We used to just offer hamburgers, sausage links, spaghetti, you know the kind of stuff anyone can make. Our restaurant business stunk, and we only kept it going to support the guests."

"Looks like you're doing well now."

"Yes," Rex grinned, "you know, only about a thousand people live within a twenty-minute drive of this place. We're now a place most people like to come for their weekly meal out."

Back home, Clint ate out on the average of five days a week, but he had a hundred nearby choices.

"How far away is your place?"

"Actually, I live here now. Long story. I like it here. I stay busy, plenty of company, I enjoy the outdoors, and I even have free internet. There's three of us who live here, although I think Jack, the young guy who works the dock may be leaving soon. And Jolene, she's been here longer than me. Used to be a high school counselor in Vancouver but got burned out. She's a nice person, runs housekeeping. You got a personal problem, talk to her. She's been a lot of help to me."

Clint liked Rex, but he didn't have any interest in hearing Rex's long story. They talked for a few more minutes, before Clint excused himself and returned to his room. Later, in bed, he wondered how things were going for Frankie and fought the urge to call her. He would give her a few more days to let things settle in Las Vegas. In the morning, he would ask around and see where the deep fishing holes were. He would also ask how to best catch the big ones. While he had done plenty of fishing in his life, he still considered himself an amateur.

CHAPTER 21

B uzz knocked on Theresa Deer's open door and walked in. "Things have only gotten worse."

"How could they?"

"The message traffic this morning is going crazy. I think the President might even get involved."

"That won't do any good," Deer said, "but my sources tell me there will be a special security council meeting today. The Chinese have overstepped themselves this time, or should I say again. The FBI is convinced they are involved in the disappearance of one of their agents and that policewoman. The Chinese are denying it, of course."

"The same day that happened, seven charter jets, each carrying a small contingent of Chinese tourists, wealthy ones, arrived in the U.S. One passenger from each has since disappeared. Three of these planes flew in from different Canadian airports and three from Mexico. One came in from Jamaica," Buzz said.

Deer knew all this but let Buzz continue. "And?"

"Facial recognition has identified two of the disappeared as known Chinese operatives, supposedly dangerous ones. More in the line of assassins than just spies is how I take that. CIA believes the others are likely the same type. The best guess is that they are here to clean up the mess and do away with any loose ends. Along that vein, this morning Las Vegas police found seven members of the Demons, the gang in Las Vegas involved with the attack on Clint, shot dead."

"I could see how the FBI thinks the Chinese took their agent."

"With Agent North and Frankie gone, that only leaves Clint left to testify. I know that's not the right word in this case, but you know what I mean."

"Have the FBI or anyone else been able to develop any leads toward what may have happened to the two?" Deer asked.

"Possibly. The white van has not been found, but they can place it traveling away from the city on a county road that goes about fifty miles out into the desert and then simply ends. They have other vehicles returning on that road, but so far have only been able to contact a few of those cars' owners. They are pursuing one interesting lead that claims a twin-engine airplane landed on an old airstrip on some abandoned property just off the road around the time the van was driving on it."

"Big enough to carry off the van?"

"No, the type of plane they think it was can carry a half dozen or so passengers but nothing as large as even a small car."

Deer had not heard about the plane. "Is there any flight record or other data out there that indicates where the plane came from or where it went?"

"None at all, and that has the FBI divided on whether the info is true or not. They are working right now at trying to find any radar data that picked it up. A plane staying low enough may not be caught on radar, but how long can a plane fly low without attracting a lot of attention?"

"It's all fascinating, but I don't see anything in it to cause us to get involved. Let's don't even address it in any of the analytical reporting we do," Deer said.

"Fine by me," Buzz said and stood up to leave the room.

"Keep an ear to it, though, Buzz. This is interesting."

After Buzz left, Deer pulled up a map of the Las Vegas area that included all the licensed airfields. She smiled when her theory proved possible. There were two private airfields within a dozen or so miles from where she thought the van was last seen. Both could be reached without flying over any of the mountains that surrounded the city. The plane may have only been in the air ten minutes and could have flown low that far without drawing too much attention. She knew her theory had flaws, and she only guessed to which road Buzz had referred, but it would be an easy solution. She would mention it to Buzz later.

Deer checked one of her hunters she had dispatched to Kenya. This one had been with her since the beginning, and she had total faith in him, but the mission was near impossible. Mission impossible, she thought, and smiled. Africa has a handful of warring tribes and many more that just didn't like each other. One particularly ruthless rebel leader had allegedly gotten ahold of an unknown quantity of the Ebola virus and was threatening to release it in an urban area, possibly Nairobi.

She thought the claim would turn out false, but there had been a break-in and a fire at a large medical research facility in South Africa the year before. An unconfirmed rumor had it that Ebola was being studied there, and some of the virus may have been removed before the fire. The Brits and the CIA had teams in Africa working with the locals to try to find any trace of the Ebola and the tribal leader making the threat. As far as she could tell, they had had no success.

Her hunter would stay in or near his hotel unless things hit the fan. He called it a vacation, and Deer hoped it would just be a waste of time. Let the CIA or the Brits solve this problem.

She stayed late at the office, and when she got up to leave, her shoulder and back reminded her she needed to move about more. Even though she had two years before she would hit the big five-o, she felt like her body had jumped ahead a dozen years, and since the injuries she sustained in Korea the year before, her exercise routine had disappeared.

Stopping in the restroom on the way out of the building, she took a long look at herself in the mirror. She had put on a few pounds in the last year, too.

"So how are we going to fix this?" she said to her reflection in the mirror.

"Oh hi, Ms. Deer," a thirtyish agent with the Marshal Service said as she entered the restroom. "What do you need to fix?"

"Hey, Margie," she had run into Margie several times in the past year, often here in the restroom. Margie had kind of a bob haircut and a permanent smile on her face.

"I've let myself fall apart. Ten pounds heavier than I need to be and out of shape. I used to have a regular exercise routine. Believe me, getting old sucks."

"You're not old," Margie said, laughing. "Most of the guys I work with think you're hot."

"Thank you for saying that, but if they really think that, it's probably because they haven't gotten a close look at me lately."

"I know you had that accident last year. That kicked you out of your routine. You can get started again. Maybe you just need a new man in your life. That always motivated me to get in shape."

"I wish, but I don't even have the energy to try to start a relationship."

"You know what they say. Good things happen when you least expect it," Margie said and disappeared inside a stall.

"Thanks, Margie, take care," Deer said and left.

She drove home, thinking about her conversation with Margie. How was she supposed to meet a man? She couldn't think of anyone with whom she associated through her work. She had no interest in online dating services or going alone to a bar. Most of her lady friends were already matched up or had already given up. Maybe she should just resign herself to this latter category.

She pulled into her driveway and stopped. She would normally drive into the garage, but a neighbor was walking a puppy and had stopped on the sidewalk in front of her house under the street light.

"Frank, is that a new dog?" she asked, immediately realizing it was a dumb question. Of course, it was. Frank lived three houses down the road and had lost his wife to cancer about a year ago. She hadn't seen the dog before, and the dog couldn't be very old.

"Yes, it's mostly a collie, I think."

"A name?" Deer asked as she squatted down to pet the dog.

"Sleepy, but I didn't name it."

"Hey, Sleepy," she said.

The puppy almost leapt into her out stretched hands. "Aren't you a friendly one. How did you get it?"

"My daughter thought I needed it. I disagreed, but in the last couple of days, he has kind of grown on me."

"If I ever get to retire, I may have to get one, too. I've always liked dogs," Deer said.

"You're way too young to even start thinking about retirement."

"Not that young, Frank."

"Guess, we'll turn around and head home. If we go too far, he makes me carry him home. Hope we see you again, I think Sleepy likes you."

"Anytime," Deer said and went into her house feeling a little better about herself.

CHAPTER 22

B uzz kept one eye on the monitor on the left. He had three set up on his desk, usually using the middle one for whatever he was currently working. The other two monitored the various feeds he had coming in from the intelligence community, international news outlets, or anything else in which he had an interest.

At two in the afternoon, the one on the left grabbed his full attention. "Crap!" he said loud enough to get Dolly's attention.

"What now?" she asked. Her desk, situated across the office, had its own set of three monitors.

"Come take a look at this," he said.

She came over and leaned over his shoulder. "How many people died?"

"Not sure," he said and scrolled through the entire message. "The van was booby trapped. Although this is preliminary reporting, sounds like at least three or four."

"Better give the boss a heads up," Dolly said.

"You want to ask her to come out here. Might be easier for her to just read this."

Dolly went into Deer's office and came out a second later. "She wants us to get everything we can on it and come brief her in fifteen minutes. I'll check the local press bulletins and screen any state reporting, if you'll take the classified feeds."

"Okay," he said and started digging through the various spot reporting and flash messages that had already started appearing within the intelligence and law enforcement community.

Fifteen minutes later, he and Dolly sat across from Deer in her office.

"What do we have?"

Buzz spoke first. "A team of FBI agents and sheriff's deputies found the white van in an old barn not too far from where it was last seen. The place looked deserted, so they called in a forensic team. Before the crime scene guys arrived, someone noticed that there was a person in the van. They got the go ahead to check if the person was alive and, if so, needed medical help. When they opened the van's rear door, there was a massive explosion. The assumption is, of course, that the van was booby trapped."

"Survivors?" Deer asked.

"One, a deputy who wasn't near the van. He was hurt, but it sounds like he'll survive."

"Have they been able to identify who was in the van?"

"Not for sure, but from the initial sighting, they thought it might have been the agent," Buzz said.

"Damn, the FBI is going to be furious."

"And rightly so," Dolly added.

"The press, the police, and the state really don't know anything more and likely not as much at this time. The whole area has been sealed off."

"Find out if anyone filed a flight plan on the day the agent was kidnapped and flew out of any functioning airfield within fifteen miles of the spot where they found the van. I'm thinking someone could have flown low for that long without raising too much suspicion. They could have filed a legitimate flight plan and gone anywhere. If there's no direct way to drive from the location of the explosion to these other airfields that would be even better."

"Private small airfields, too?" Dolly asked.

"Yes, they would be the best fit."

"Makes sense, do you think the FBI is looking at that?" Buzz asked.

"I would hope so. Wonder what happened to the woman?" Deer said.

"She's probably dead or will be dead soon," Buzz said.

Both Deer and Dolly nodded.

"They're a bunch of asshole men," Dolly said. "They may not be in a hurry to kill her. If Clint hears about this, it may be hard to restrain him."

Deer looked at Buzz. He nodded.

"Don't pass on anything to him," Deer said and sent them back to their desks to continue monitoring the situation.

Deer contemplated making a phone call to one of the senior agents at the FBI national headquarters but decided to hold off until the incident hit the news. Then she could pass along her condolences and dig for anything new.

In less than five minutes, Dolly and Buzz were back in her office. "You were right," Buzz said. "A Cessna 340A took off from a private field about twelve miles south of where the explosion took place with a destination of Eugene, Oregon. Supposedly only the pilot was on the airplane."

"That's what the flight plan says?"

"Yes," Buzz replied. "Not hard to lie about that. Think it was them?"

"If I was them, I'd have the pilot say he was just going to take the plane out for a quick test flight or something and be right back. You know say something about wanting the plane to be functioning well before going on a long trip. I'd make a big thing about being alone, even have someone come on board to do something and be able to later state that no one else was on the plane," Deer said.

"Then fly out pick everyone up and fly right back," Buzz said.

Deer nodded. "Have the sun visors down, so no one could see in. Fuel up and take off again."

"I bet you're right. Do we need to do anything to make sure the FBI is pursuing this possibility?" Dolly asked.

"No, they'll think of it. They may already be chasing down that plane. However, let's see what we can find out about the pilot and what happened after the plane landed."

"I imagine they'll do another switch of some sort in Eugene. Maybe get in a van and go to Portland International and fly out of there in some charter jet. May be impossible to keep tracking them," Buzz said.

"They may already be back in China by now," Deer said.

CHAPTER 23

Frankie fought to clear the heavy fog away from her mind. Most of her wanted to go back to sleep, but enough fear had reached her consciousness to get her attention. She needed answers. Where was she and what was happening? A loud constant noise and a steady vibration gave her something on which to focus.

She opened her eyes, but all she could see was a carpeted floor and a wall inches from her face. The memory of the attack outside the bakery slowly came back to her, but she remembered nothing since. Agent North had been with her, and she wondered if he was nearby. She wanted to move and to look around, but her muscles wouldn't respond. She resisted panicking and listened for any clues that might give her some idea of what was happening.

She lay there listening and thought she might have heard something in a foreign language, but the constant sound of the aircraft engines and the drugs in her system soon pushed her back to sleep. Twenty minutes before the plane landed in Eugene, a petite Chinese woman injected another dose of sedative into her. Frankie's eyes fluttered briefly as the needle penetrated her skin. She saw the woman's profile before she drifted back into the darkness. Later she would wonder if what she saw was a dream. Regardless, the image of a Chinese woman became the key in her mind to unraveling her situation.

It didn't happen right away. Frankie slept for four hours, and the next time she woke up, it took her a few minutes to think straight. She was no longer laying on the floor but was belted into a chair. Everything tilted to the right and with that motion, Frankie realized she was on an airplane. The sudden realization of where she was brought relief and fear at the same time.

Her mind began to clear and the vision of the woman leaning over and sticking her in the leg answered another question. She had been drugged. She wondered how long she had been out. When she tried to lift her arm to look at her watch, she discovered her wrists had been taped to the rails of the wheel chair she now occupied. The chair was bolted to a metal bar on the floor.

Looking around, she could see she was in the cargo compartment of the airplane. A dozen suitcases surrounded her. She couldn't make out a lot as the only light in the room came from moonlight that flowed in through two small round windows, one on each side of the plane. A nightlight of some sort also lit up the area around the door that most likely led to the main cabin. Frankie considered the size of the baggage compartment and the width of the airplane and guessed the airplane to be the size of a small commuter plane. She listened to the engines and decided they were jet engines and close by.

She didn't see Agent North and had a bad feeling he was already dead. She wondered why she was still alive and where she was being taken. The vision of the Asian looking woman came back to her.

"Chinese," she said out loud and instinctively looked around again to see if anyone heard her. She remembered the Chinese involvement in the shootout, and Clint explaining something about the Chinese buying up property near Nellis Air Force Base.

Were they taking her to China? What for? She had nothing to tell anyone. Why waste the time taking her anywhere when they could've already killed her. A thought popped into her mind that she refused to acknowledge, but it wouldn't go away. Human trafficking? Fear raced through her.

"Not me, not me," she whispered and felt tears form in her eyes.

She couldn't reach up to wipe her eyes, but her self-pity didn't last long. Anger replaced it and hardened her. If given a chance, she would survive whatever they did to her and at some point, she would have her revenge. She would survive, and she would get back home.

Her head hurt, and her mouth was dry, but she didn't want company, so she remained silent. Someone would come at some point to check on her or to take her somewhere else. Maybe they would let her know why they had kidnapped her and what happened to Phil.

She hoped they wouldn't sedate her again.

CHAPTER 24

Five days after the van explosion outside Las Vegas, Buzz walked into Theresa Deer's office.

"Boss, some things are finally falling together with this Chinese matter."

"There are dozens of Chinese matters. You are talking about Clint's Chinese matter, I assume."

"Yes. The FBI is doing a good job in putting the pieces of the puzzle together. A lot of money has been seized or accounts frozen, land by the bases is in the process of being seized by the government, and they have traced a group of people from Las Vegas to Anchorage, Alaska. From there, everything gets a little messy."

"What do you mean, messy?"

"Everyone left the airplane in Anchorage, got into different taxis and went to different places."

"The plane?"

"Flew onto China, via Japan."

"No passengers."

"That's right, boss. Records in Alaska and Japan verify just that. The plane even spent a night in Japan. Security footage shows no one getting on or off, and there was ground crew that boarded the plane in Japan."

"So, everyone stayed in Alaska or caught a subsequent plane," Deer said.

"It seems so."

"Walk me through how they're so sure the plane took our

suspects to Alaska."

"Well, despite the initial claim that no passengers were on board when the first plane left Nevada, seven passengers got off the plane in Eugene, Oregon. A rental van took the seven directly to Portland where they boarded a larger charter jet for Anchorage. Best we can tell all seven passengers boarded the jet. And, listen to this, one of the passengers was a female invalid in a wheel chair. Security footage is not that clear, but the woman in the wheel chair appears to be our missing police officer."

"Interesting. Any ID on the others?"

"Not from the manifest. The FBI is pretty sure all the names are false. Facial recognition is no good either as no one went through customs anywhere; however, the FBI believes three of the men are part of the contingent that arrived in separate flights about a week ago."

"I remember," Deer said. "So, they're done here. That's good. What does the rental van driver say about the passengers?"

"They haven't located him yet."

"Not good."

"The police woman got off in Anchorage, too?"

Buzz wanted to call her Frankie, but stayed with the impersonal. "Yes, she was in a wheelchair and appeared unconscious."

"Creepy asses."

"The FBI is working with the locals in Anchorage to try to find everyone now."

"Have you been there?" Deer asked.

"Anchorage?"

"Not that big of a city, but leave it and in an hour, you're in the middle of nowhere. Alaska is an easy place to disappear."

"I saw something on television once on how a lot of criminals and divorced husbands who want to get out of paying child support have fled to Alaska to disappear," Buzz said.

Deer nodded. "Is the FBI having any success tracking them in Alaska?"

"Not that I've been able to gather. I've run a trace for any places or people of interest to the intelligence community. There are more there than I would've thought. Meaning Alaska, not just Anchorage."

"Anything looking good for this?"

"Not that I can see."

"Hopefully, local law enforcement will have a better feel for all this, but I think more blood will be shed before this is all over. The Chinese won't go quietly."

"Do we want to send anyone there?" Buzz asked.

"No, this is bad, but it doesn't warrant our involvement. Just keep monitoring the situation, it could get out of hand. Don't talk to Clint about this. If he calls about it, pass him to me."

Buzz returned to the outer office. Dolly looked up at him. She was wearing a dark blue blouse and had one more button unfastened than she should have in Buzz mind. He knew he was old fashioned and a bit of a prude, as she would say, but he also knew she liked teasing him, which she did a lot. She would button this one button if she left the office or went in to talk to the boss.

Buzz liked Dolly, and the feeling he believed was mutual,

but there was no sexual attraction. They worked well together and had each other's back when things got hectic. If pushed, he might classify her as a friend, and he didn't have many. Where he might proudly describe himself as old fashioned and straitlaced, Dolly seemed to enjoy giving him the impression that she had the morals of an alley cat. He knew that she knew that some of her comments and behavior embarrassed him, and he was pretty sure that was the reason she behaved like she did in the office around him. On the occasions they were together outside the office and among others, he thought she behaved like a lady should.

Dolly wouldn't need to be pushed to claim Buzz as a friend. She liked him and admired his work ethic. She also liked the way he treated her. He reminded her of a proper English gentleman as portrayed in any one of the several British television shows she enjoyed watching. Early on in their association, she had brought up a movie she had gone to over the weekend that had a lot of sex in it. She had mentioned that she would've loved being in one of the more intimate scenes with the young male actor and asked Buzz if ever fantasized being with some female star. Buzz talked around the question and blushed quite noticeably.

Since then, Dolly couldn't resist teasing the poor man. She believed she had a healthy, open outlook on sex and only portrayed herself as a loose woman around Buzz to get a reaction. At times, she had even felt a little guilty about it, but she continued.

"What did she say?" Dolly asked.

"We monitor it, but stay out of it."

"I almost feel guilty that we're not telling Clint that his lady friend has been kidnapped and may be just across the border from him."

"Me, too," Buzz said. "She's a nice lady. If they're keeping her alive, it can only be for one reason that I can think of."

"To give to someone as a gift," Dolly said. "Common practice in the old days and in the underworld today. He may be really pissed at us when he finds out what has happened."

Buzz nodded. "The fact that she's missing is already on the news. He'll surely find out soon enough."

"Did she specifically tell you not to tell him?"

"Yes."

"Any bets on when he might be calling in and asking us why?"

"No. Let's hope she's rescued before that happens."

Buzz was just about to close up and go home when the message traffic went crazy. He glanced at it for a second before jumping up, motioning to Dolly, and going into Deer's office.

"Something's going down. The FBI and Alaskan State police are raiding a camp about eighty miles outside Anchorage."

CHAPTER 25

Frankie's head throbbed but the nausea had passed. The small room smelled, and she believed most of the odor came from her. She had lost track of time. What had it been, three or four days since she arrived here?

One low wattage bulb, screwed into the ceiling without any covering produced enough light to see around the room. She believed it was some type of meat or fish processing room. No more than ten feet by ten feet, other than the one light and a large sink with a counter, the room was empty.

She stood up and walked around the room, feeling more aware of her surroundings than at any time since she was kidnapped. She hoped this was a sign that they would stop drugging her. Thinking this, she felt relieved that whatever sedative they were using must not be addictive because she had no desire to receive another shot.

They had dressed her in what her grandmother would have referred to as a moo-moo. A long, dark brown, one-piece dress that went from her shoulders to below her knees. She had no shoes on her feet, and to her embarrassment had nothing on underneath the dress. Her mind flashed vague visions of men doing terrible things to her while she was unconscious, and she told herself that was only her imagination. Nightmares, that was all they were. She would keep telling herself that.

Where was she? She couldn't recall traveling anywhere after being on the airplane. If she could only look out a window.

The door to the room was locked, but the faucet in the sink worked, and she splashed some cold water on her face. It felt good. She let the water run over her arms before drying them on the dress she wore. She lifted the dress and dried her face, only to be struck with a nasty odor.

"Dammit!" She shouted. "Well Frankie, let's hope it's at least yours."

She began thinking how she could take her revenge on her kidnappers when she heard shouting outside. Instinctively, she froze and listened, but the shouting turned into gunfire and a lot of it. With no place to hide, Frankie lay back down on the floor and hoped no stray rounds would fine her there. It only made sense that someone was trying to rescue her. She thought of Clint and hoped, if he was out there, he wouldn't be hurt.

The shooting lasted for a full minute, maybe two. The thought came to her that it sounded like an actual wartime battle. She believed she heard someone screaming in pain. Finally, the gunfire stopped.

Was it over, she wondered? Had she been rescued? She wanted to yell, to let them know where she was, but for the moment she waited silently. She heard a single shot in the distance and wondered how many people died in the last few minutes.

A man started shouting, and she thought the person was calling out names. She didn't hear responses.

"I'm in here!" she shouted and started banging on the door. Frustrated, she looked around the room again in a futile hope she had missed something earlier that she could now use to make more of a racket banging on the door.

No one came for her despite her shouting, and she began to

worry that maybe they couldn't find her. Time went by. Where was everyone? Then she had a horrible thought, was the room underground hidden from view?

"Hold on," someone finally said something from outside the room.

Relieved, she smiled. "Finally," she said.

She heard a key being inserted into the door, and the door swung open. She had been standing by the door and took a step back. The man she had not seen before stood on the other side. His appearance startled her; he was huge, maybe six foot six, she thought. He had short red hair and an unkempt reddish beard. His nose had been scarred long ago. He took one step into the room and without warning slugged her in the face. She felt her jaw give as her knees buckled.

The next thing she remembered was being on the floor of another damn airplane. Her hands were tied behind her back and her head hurt like hell. She felt like her mouth had been taped shut. The plane bumped up and down in rough winds, and Frankie wished for the first time in years that she could just die.

CHAPTER 26

Clint had finished packing his few items in his car and had entered the restaurant to get a coffee to go when Buzz called him.

"Can you talk?" Buzz asked.

"Yes, what's up?"

"We need you to come off your vacation."

"Alright, what's going on?" Clint asked, feeling like Buzz was being hesitant.

"It all goes back to Las Vegas. Things have gone to hell."

"Is there a reason you're not getting to the point?"

"They've got Frankie, Clint. They grabbed her and Agent North off the street in Las Vegas. They killed North, but we believe they took Frankie with them when they left the city."

Clint sat down at an empty table. "Where do they have her?" The server came over with his coffee, and Clint nodded a thank you.

"At the moment we're not sure, and Clint, her disappearance is not the reason I'm calling. We don't send hunters out to save a person in danger. It's not practical. People are in danger everyday everywhere."

"Get to the point, Buzz, why are you calling me?" Clint tried to keep his frustration out of his voice.

"There's been a major screwup, but let me go back to the beginning." Buzz briefed him on the kidnapping, the discovery of the van and the explosion killing the agents and deputies in Nevada. He told Buzz how they had tracked the group to a remote hunting camp in Alaska."

"And you believe Frankie was the woman in the wheel chair?"

"Yes, we're pretty certain, but we don't know why they would have any interest in taking her anywhere. But let me bring you up to speed as to why the boss now thinks we should get involved. A team of FBI agents and Alaskan State Police officers raided the camp outside Anchorage late yesterday afternoon. They merged on the camp in five vehicles. A police helicopter was supposed to be there, too, but had mechanical problems and turned back."

"Did they find Frankie?" Clint asked.

"We don't know what happened, but all the good guys were killed or are missing. It appears there was a major gun battle. The FBI and the state have a major league, forensic task force there right now trying to put everything together, but it's going to be a slow, long process. Apparently, all the bodies were taken into the largest structure there, a big log cabin, and the place was set on fire, professionally. The whole cabin burned down with the bodies inside."

"Think any were burned alive?"

"Hope not."

"Any of the bodies female?" Clint asked.

"Too soon to know. At this point they're trying to keep everything out of the press. This was a major screw up, and besides, there are a lot of next to kin notifications to be made."

"What's this got to do with us or me?"

"Two things." Buzz paused for a minute, and Clint wondered if he was reading something or listening to someone else. "First, the FBI and the state are recoiling like they've been snake bit. They've taken on a defensive posture, more concerned with getting to the bottom of this and not making another mistake, than continuing the chase. Second, it's obvious that somehow the bad guys won the gun battle, and the survivors have disappeared."

"Any guesses how they got away or how many did?"

"Seems like they must have made their escape on boat or plane. A second team of state police and wildlife agents were sent out after the helicopter had to turn around. They got there about forty-five minutes or so after the original team. The last twenty minutes is down a backroad that's not busy. In fact, they passed no one coming from the camp on the road, and we don't believe they could have gotten out by road any quicker."

"I'm assuming the camp had boats they could use, but an airplane?"

"We think yes to the plane and know there were boats there. Three were still there. They're trying to find out if there were more. It's a crap shoot at the moment. One of the wildlife agents who got there in the first vehicle to arrive said she thought she heard an airplane in the distance. No one else heard it, and she didn't mention it to anyone at the time. The large cabin was on fire, and they could see blood on and around one of the police cars already there."

"I imagine their first thought was to secure the area, thinking the shooters might still be around," Clint said and remembered clearing the scene of an explosion when he was in the military.

"They called for firetrucks and crime scene investigators right away and slowly searched the grounds. It wasn't until the firemen had arrived, and the fire had subsided, that they found the bodies. I think they're still finding them as we talk."

"What am I supposed to do?"

"Start driving to Alaska, you're almost there already. We'll have some more info for you later today. Deer is trying to figure if there was a plane, where they could have gone. Dolly is working the boat angle. I'm glued to the computer while trying to get my contacts at the FBI and DHS to talk to me. Luckily this is of high importance to the Marshal Service, too."

"Are we thinking the Chinese are still involved?"

"Yes."

"And best guess about Frankie?"

"That she's alive, Clint. She's their prisoner and would have had no reason to have been involved in the shooting. If they took her that far, I can't see why they wouldn't have taken her with them when they left."

"I hope you're right. I'm already packed and will be on the road in five minutes. Stay in touch." Clint knew the odds were low that Frankie was still alive, despite what Buzz had said. If the survivors of the shootout knew they had to make a quick getaway, why not just shoot their prisoner and leave. How much value could she have to them?

He backed out of the lodge's parking lot and waved at the manager who stood on the large porch, waving at him. "Maybe I'll come back," Clint said to himself. He started driving and noticed the navigation instructions had already been set in his car. It was going to be a very long drive.

In the small, nearby town of Burns Lake, Clint gassed the car and grabbed a bag of groceries to eat in the car. He wasn't hungry now, but he knew driving north there wouldn't be many places to stop. He withdrew a hundred dollars cash from an ATM in the store before leaving.

His mind drifted to possible scenarios for a gunfight between eight or so trained law enforcement personnel and a group of individuals. His first thought was that they had to have been outnumbered and outgunned. However, he knew from his past, if proper defensive positions are set up and with the smallest amount of advanced warning, a disciplined group can do a lot of damage. This part of Canada had a million trees, and he suspected Alaska wasn't much different. Just one sniper position in the trees would be a huge threat to a group of people in a relatively open space.

Clint needed a rifle but being unfamiliar with Canada's gun laws, he decided to wait until reaching Alaska to purchase one. Night vision goggles would be handy, too, and maybe some hunting clothes. Traipsing around the Alaskan bush in blue jeans and a tee shirt wouldn't be a good way to stay unnoticed.

He started to think about Frankie, but just as quickly forced himself to put her out of his mind. He didn't need to start thinking what they could be doing to her. If he was to succeed in rescuing her, if that was even going to be a possibility, he needed to approach this cold blooded and calculated.

Stopping after a couple hours for gas and a break, Clint checked the navigation settings to find out where they were sending him. He wasn't surprised to discover the settings only took him to a highway intersection outside Anchorage. Buzz had told him they weren't sure where Frankie may have been taken, but he knew they were working hard at pinpointing a location. If they came up with one, new settings would be put in. If they didn't, he'd likely end up at a hotel around Anchorage. He would be patient; he would have to be as the drive would take a very long two days.

CHAPTER 27

Clint had reached the intersection with Alaskan Highway in the Yukon territories after a very slow and scenic drive up Highway 37 when the phone interrupted his drive.

"We need you to turn around," Deer said.

"Is it over?"

"No, but if I'm right, they're closer to you than they were. We're putting new coordinates in your car. You need to go to Skagway. Don't try to get there tonight. Tomorrow is fine, plus I still have to work on a few things."

"How did they get there?" He remembered hearing something about Skagway before and thought it was in Alaska.

"If my theory is correct, by plane. The camp had one of those planes that takes off and lands at lakes. It can hold a total of six people. They would've had to refuel, but I imagine that would've been easy with all the places up there."

"Anyone arrested and talking to the police yet?"

"In Vegas very little has been developed, and in Alaska, nothing. The theory is some left the Alaskan site by plane and maybe some left by boat. Of course, no one has any idea how many got away. There's reason to believe one of the fishing boats is missing. We know the plane is. No flight plan was coordinated with the FAA or air traffic control, but apparently that's not uncommon in Alaska."

"Anything developed from the fire?" Clint asked.

"Not yet. Listen, Clint, I just want you there as a last resort. I'm worried things may move quickly and the FBI and Alaskan state authorities will want to act more cautiously this time. I can't blame them, but there may not be much time."

"Before what?"

"They all disappear back to China. I'm surprised they haven't already."

"Can't be too many of them left to go back."

"We need a couple to link them with their American supporters. We being the primarily FBI, but the entire intelligence community is interested in this. I don't know if anyone else has reached a conclusion like mine that puts these people near Skagway, but the FBI will at some point or at least should."

"I'll be on the road first thing in the morning. Anything else?"

"No."

Clint followed a billboard's directions to a hotel only a few miles away near the city of Whitehorse. He had hoped Deer could have given him some insight into whether Frankie was alive or not. He hoped she wasn't holding anything back from him and didn't think she would. Stay cool, he reminded himself.

The next morning, he crossed the border into Alaska with barely any delay and stopped at the small Alaskan welcome center to get gas and take a welcome break from driving. The drive wasn't that long but the winding, mountainous roads made him pay attention. Wildlife and big trucks popped up when least expected. Once he thought he saw a bear hustle off the road as he came over a small hilltop. The town of Skagway was small and looked more rural than urban, even downtown.

A lot of people were walking around, and Clint wondered

if they were tourists, and if so, what was the draw here. He parked and entered Rudolph's Diner, which was not crowded, and sat at a table in the middle of the room. An older, heavy-set man wearing overalls and a large apron approached him.

"Morning, what can I get you?"

"What do you recommend?" Clint asked.

"We're still serving breakfast, and the steak and eggs are great, but if you're looking for lunch, I recommend the moose burger. We're famous for it."

"Let's go with the moose burger," Clint said and wondered how famous they really were.

"With fries?"

"Sure, and a diet coke."

Clint knew he didn't need to check in, but he wanted the latest Section had before he started doing anything in this small town. He called the office and Dolly answered.

"Hi, Clint, how are you doing?"

"Fine so far, I'm here in Skagway."

"Something's happening right now. Can we call you back in a few?"

"Yes, I'm just looking for the latest."

"It won't be long," Dolly said and ended the call.

Clint used his phone to search for any mention of Frankie in the Las Vegas press releases and found several articles from the local paper and local news channels. They all described what a great person she was, how the LVPD praised her, and how everyone hoped she would be found safe. None of the articles mentioned him, but the FBI agent, Phil North was mentioned several times.

"Here you go," the server said and placed the burger in

front of him. "Hope it's enough for you."

Clint grinned. The moose burger included at least a half-pound of meat on a large bun. A pile of condiments sat next to it, and a stack of large, wedge cut fries spilled out over a red, plastic basket. Steam could still be seen coming off the burger. "I think it will be just fine."

"Where are you from?"

"You don't think I'm native?"

"You live here as long as I have, and you pretty much come to know all the locals."

"Texas, although I've been known to move around a bit. Are all these people wondering around outside tourists?"

"Yes, most all of them off the cruise ships. We don't get many normal tourists."

"The cruise ships, I should have thought about that. I didn't think many would come the way I did," Clint said.

"You drove? What for?" he laughed. "Almost no one drives here. My name's Eric, can I join you for a moment?"

"Yes. A couple of things brought me here, but nothing specific. I enjoy heading out to points less traveled. Besides, I'm trying to write the great American novel, and I've been getting nowhere for a while, so, I thought a trip could help clear my mind."

"An author, now that's interesting. I've never known one."

"Well, you still don't. I've got nothing published. I guess that way I can still call myself a starving artist."

"Known lots of those," Eric said and grinned.

"I spent the last several days fishing at Lake Babine in B.C."

"I know it. Better fishing around here though. We've got lakes you can catch fish without bait." A customer entered the restaurant, and Eric stood up. "I'll catch you later, the lunch crowd is starting to show up."

Clint watched him greet the couple that entered and wondered if the place ever really got crowded. He took a bite of his moose burger and had to admit it was quite good. He covered the mountain of French fries with ketchup and continued eating. Eric brought him a drink refill without having to be asked.

"Come back for breakfast. You'll be impressed with our moose sausage and blueberry pancakes," Eric said when he dropped off the check.

"I will." Clint was a little surprised by the high price for his lunch, but he imagined everything might be expensive in Skagway.

He decided to leave his car parked outside the restaurant and explore Skagway by foot. After about thirty minutes, he thought he had covered most of the downtown area and had decided without the tourist trade the town would be half the size if not smaller. He followed a sign that said cruise ships and saw the large Princess Cruise Line ship docked at the port. People drifted on and off the ship in no hurry to get anywhere. The good life, he thought.

He glanced at his phone but had no messages. A cool north wind had picked up speed and put a chill in the air. Dark clouds were drifting south over the mountain tops, threatening to block the sunshine, and Clint hoped they weren't bringing anything ominous with them.

CHAPTER 28

"This is where you'll be staying for the next few days. You'll meet Chappie today or tomorrow. You already met Red at your last stop. The big guy with a red beard. Well, Chappie is his big brother, and as long as you can keep him happy, you'll stay alive. Hope you do better than the last one." The man doing the talking had greasy black hair and looked like a rat. Shorter than Frankie and missing two fingers on his left hand, he had been the only person she had seen since being hit in the face in her last private cell. By the time he had come and taken her off the airplane, everyone else was gone.

Frankie stared at him and tried to say something through the tape over her mouth. Rat Face yanked the tape off, and Frankie gasped. She felt like one layer of skin, if not more, came off with the tape.

"Let me go," her voice cracked and was almost unrecognizable to her. "Why are you doing this?"

"Hey, you should be thankful. The only reason you're alive is that they decided giving you as a gift to Chappie was a better plan than just killing you. They wanted points with the big man. Everyone does."

Frankie didn't need much of an imagination to know what was going on. "Can you bring me a glass of water and something to eat?"

"Not me, not on my list of chores."

"How about at least cut my hands free."

Rat Face walked out and closed the door without replying.

Frankie walked around the room. Every part of her body hurt, especially her head. She opened her mouth as wide as she could and moved her jaw around slowly. The left side of her jaw ached and felt swollen, but she didn't think anything was broken. The room had four walls, no windows, and no sink. A mattress that looked disgusting lay on the floor, and a bucket sat in the corner.

She felt like crying but didn't have any tears left. Wearing the same, smelly, soiled dress that she had worn for the last couple of days, she didn't see how they expected her to make a good impression on Chappie. If she had a rope and a hook available in the ceiling, she would hang herself.

"No, you wouldn't," she said out loud to the empty room. "You will find a way to kill every one of these slimy bastards. You will survive this. Besides, maybe this Chappie jerk likes his women smelly." This made her laugh for a second, but then the reality of her situation set in.

She had no sense of time, which she found frustrating, and it seemed like hours before anyone came to her room. This time Rat Face came with a woman that could have been his twin sister. Frankie had a thought that these two could play crew members on an old pirate ship in a movie. The woman looked like she made little, if any, effort to make herself presentable.

She walked around Frankie, clucking to herself. "Okay," she said. "We'll be back in a few minutes to get you cleaned up." The two left, and true to her word, they returned in a few minutes.

"Come with me," the woman said.

"Who are you?" Frankie asked as politely as she could manage, not being in any mood to be polite.

"I'm Jan. You need anything here you can ask me." She grasped Frankie's elbow and led her out of the room and down a windowless hall that led into a larger, open room. "This is where they clean the fish, but they're not using it right now, so we can. Now I'm going to cut your hands free. You make any sudden moves, and I'll stab you."

"And then I'll shoot you," Rat Face said.

Frankie saw he had a small revolver pointed at her. A thirty-eight, she thought, big enough to kill.

Jan sliced through the tape without much effort. "Take off that thing you're wearing," Jan ordered, stepping away from her.

Frankie didn't hesitate. Her hands felt numb but worked. She held the dress off to the side and dropped it onto the floor, glad to be rid of it. She saw but ignored Rat Face leering at her.

"Don't get all worked up," Jan said to Rat Face. "Only chance you have at this is when Chappie tires of her and passes her onto the rest of you guys, and even then, you know you won't be first. However, looking at her, I don't think Chappie will be in a hurry to get rid of her. Hell, girl, you could set a new record. I can see why the China man brought you all this way." She said China man as two distinct words, as though it was a nickname.

The China man. Suddenly, everything clicked together. Frankie knew there had to be a reason they had spared her and brought her here, and, of course, the thought of human trafficking was always there. Now, though, she understood a lot more. This man, Chappie, was important to the Chinese. Very important, she thought, for them to take this much risk with her. She was a bonus, a tribute, maybe, that the China man thought could help reinforce his relationship with Chappie.

The cold water from the hose hit her hard, almost knocking her off her feet. She instinctively brought her forearms up to protect her face. Jan worked the hose and sprayed her until Frankie's shivering almost turned into convulsions. Rat face smiled, enjoying the show.

Jan turned the spicket on the hose off and tossed her a white, stained and torn bath towel. "Dry yourself off."

"No soap or shampoo?" Frankie said, not trying to hide her sarcasm.

"Don't get sarcastic with me and watch your tone," Jan said. She grabbed a dark blue bathrobe that looked in decent condition and tossed it to Frankie. "Drop the towel on the floor and put that on."

They led her back to the room and locked her in. With her hands now free, she rubbed her jaw and felt around her face, testing for any spots of pain and finding a few. She went to a far corner, sat down, and waited.

CHAPTER 29

The Pacific Vistas B&B didn't have a view of the Pacific Ocean like the name implied, but the bed was firm and the shower had plenty of hot water. Clint had spent two nights here, and other than walking at least five miles in hopes of seeing something that might lead him to Frankie, he had accomplished nothing. He had heard nothing from anyone at Section.

Frustrated, he decided to skip the breakfast at the Pacific Vistas and walked back to Rudolph's Diner. Eric greeted him as he entered.

"They make you work here every day?" Clint asked, smiling and shaking Eric's outstretched hand.

"Just about. You're lucky they don't make me do the cooking, too. Good timing, the breakfast crowd will be showing up soon."

Clint grinned. Only one other couple occupied a table in the restaurant. He hoped a crowd would show up for the restaurant's sake, but if the so-called lunch crowd two days earlier was any indication, there might not be much of a real crowd today either. As suggested, Clint ordered the moose sausage and blueberry pancakes.

Eric beamed. "You remembered. Good choice, you won't regret it." He went to the counter and put in Clint's order before returning.

"Where'd you choose to stay? Not too many choices but most of them aren't too bad."

"At the Pacific Vistas, not far from here."

"Know it well, Misty Stringer owns the place. She and Rudolph are second or maybe third cousins."

"This Rudolph?" Clint said and tapped the table.

"Yes sir, she's a bit younger. Rudolph just turned eighty but is still in good shape. Only hangs around here on the weekends, though. Misty stopped by a few weeks ago and had breakfast with Rudolph and a couple other members of the clan. Rudolph's younger brother owns the hardware store and one of the gas stations in town. Not the one out on the road you passed coming in. The other one just down the road." Eric pointed out a direction that didn't mean much to Clint. "As you can imagine, a lot of people here are related to each other. Turnover is small, and more people seem to be leaving than coming these days."

"Population go up and down with the cruise season?" Clint asked.

"Amazingly so and especially the younger ones."

"Is there an airport here?"

"A small one but no airlines fly into it. We do get a steady stream of small aircraft. I hear that Alaska has more pilots per capita than any other state or country in the world."

"I guess it needs them just to get around."

"A lot of the planes that fly in around here never even fly into the airport. Several just pick a lake and land. You know, they have those pontoon things. If you've never landed on a lake, you don't know what you're missing," Eric said.

"They can just do this?"

"This is Alaska. Once you are outside city limits, and I guess for airplanes not in the commercial air-lanes, there are a lot of things people get away with up here. I mean if you're a hundred miles from the nearest town and you want to land on one of the million, nameless lakes up here, why should you have to ask for permission?"

A bell rang in the back, and Eric walked away, returning a few seconds later with Clint's breakfast.

"Here it is," he said and set the platter of food in front of Clint. "More coffee?"

"Sure. By the way, with the lack of commercial flights, how do all the temporary workers leave at the end of the season?"

"Those who work for the cruise line might get free passage on a cruise ship somewhere, but the vast majority take the ferry to Juneau. Can't drive there, but once there you can fly out of the big airport."

Clint thought the term big in this case might be relative. "Not many roads leave the city?"

Eric chuckled. "Not real roads. A lot of people who live outside the city have access to the water and get around by boat. Some people get in and out by four-wheeler but not many."

A family of four came in and drew Eric away. Clint focused on his breakfast and wasn't disappointed.

Later that day, the call came in a little before four o'clock while Clint was studying the large commercial fishing pier.

"Hey, Clint, are you doing okay?" Theresa Deer asked from her office in Washington D.C.

"Just fine, anything new?"

"Nothing good, unfortunately. They somehow slipped through our fingers and got back to China."

"Who?"

Deer knew why he asked the question. "Not Frankie, Clint. We've lost track of her. Don't know if that's good or bad. Three of the key Chinese operatives we believe were involved in this got away. Although we don't know for sure, we believe two more were found in the burned building up by Anchorage. No remains of a woman were found there."

"Were these the same ones that were in Las Vegas?"

"We think two of them were on the plane that flew to Anchorage, but can't say for sure about the other one. Too much guessing with all this unfortunately, but Clint," Deer paused.

"Yes."

"I do think some of those who survived the FBI raid on the cabin by Anchorage escaped by flying down to where you are. We've traced a small plane to the area around Skagway. I say around, because we don't have a specific location. I can't say who was on the plane, and have no reason to keep you in Skagway, but if you want to stay for a few days, we'll cover your expenses while you're there."

"I might just do that."

"Good luck," Deer said and terminated the call.

Clint leaned against a light post. The air off the sea was cold and the water looked dark. An unpleasant whiff of diesel fuel drifted by him. He heard a couple crewmen arguing over something. He looked at them and the arguing turned into laughter, as one of the two did something to show the other that he was right.

He knew what Deer meant but didn't come out and say. She believed Frankie was in the area. Might be dead, might be alive, but Deer believed she was on the airplane that landed somewhere near Skagway nearly a week ago. Of course, he was already operating on that theory and had gotten nowhere.

"In town alone," a woman about his age asked.

She had walked up behind him, and while he had a glimpse of her a few seconds before, he had given her little thought.

"Isn't everybody?" he said.

"You don't have to be," she said. She had a rough look about her, and her eyes seemed sad. She wore an old, brown leather jacket with a faux fur collar. Her dark brown hair matched the color of the jacket and looked about as clean. Her eyebrows looked hairless and painted on.

"Too early for me right now," he said, guessing that she was a prostitute.

"Maybe later," she sounded anxious.

"Where do the locals hang out at night. A place with music, maybe."

She thought for a while. "The Blue House on Third Street. What's your name?"

"Clint, and yours?"

"Shayla, think you could give me some dinner money? It'll come off the price later."

Clint handed her a twenty. "Shayla, look for me at the Blue House at ten tonight, okay?"

She smiled. "I'll be there."

Clint felt sorry for her as she walked away, although he had some suspicion that he might have just been conned.

CHAPTER 30

Clint arrived at the Blue House at ten minutes before ten. Shayla was waiting for him in the shadows created by a nearby street light and the hardware store next door. She came up to him and grabbed his arm.

"Told you I'd be here," she said. She had on the same clothes, but Clint thought she had washed her hair.

"Good, let's go inside."

They entered together, and Clint paused inside to look around. The place had the atmosphere of an old-time saloon. Wooden tables spread around the room on a wooden floor that had seen better years. Two men were on stage, one at a piano and one with a guitar. The man with the guitar had a microphone in front of him. He was singing something that Clint thought could've been an old BB King tune and was pretty good.

"There's a table," Shayla pointed to an empty table not far from the stage. Clint nodded and she led him to it, never letting go of his arm.

Couples occupied most of the tables. One table had two couples and the closest one to Clint and Shayla had five men around it. A very skinny waitress followed them to the table and took their order. Clint ordered a beer and Shayla ordered a jack and coke. The waitress gave Shayla a look that Clint interpreted as being not very welcoming.

"They play old time music here, I hope that's okay," Shayla said.

"It's fine."

"They also have pretzels and chips." She looked around at the other customers, and Clint wondered if she was nervous about something.

"How long have you lived up here?" he asked.

"For years." She might have said more, but the server came back with their drinks. Shayla took hers and squeezing the glass in both hands, took a long sip. Her eyes stayed focused on her drink. Clint wondered if he had wanted to, if he had the strength to pry the glass from her grip.

"What do you do for a living?" he asked.

"Oh, I've had lots of different jobs."

"What are the people like in Skagway?"

"Like anywhere else." She drank the last of her jack and coke and sucked an ice cube into her mouth.

Well, this was a dumb plan, Clint thought. He met her here to pick her brains on the local population. He figured she had more information than most on who was doing what to whom in Skagway, and who might be dealing in serious criminal activity. He never had any intention of taking her up on anything sexual, but he did think she could give him a good lead or two to investigate.

"Could I have one more?" she asked, her eyes not meeting his.

"Yes, but I need some information, Shayla."

"Okay, that's easy," she said, but he wondered if it would be. Shayla caught the waitress' attention and pointed toward her glass.

"Do many people live outside the town?" Clint asked.

"You mean like in the mountains?"

"Yes, but along the coast, too."

"A lot of people have cabins just outside the city and there are small clusters of families that live here and there. I know some of them, the men anyways. Are you looking for someone in particular? Do you have a picture?"

The question surprised him. He had not thought about showing Frankie's picture to anyone, but decided this was not the time.

"It's not so much that I'm looking for one person, I'm looking for a group of people that might have international connections and involved in activities outside the law."

Shayla giggled. "That could be a lot of people here." Her drink arrived, and she greeted it like a long, lost friend, grasping it like the other in two hands and holding it close to her after taking a sip.

The singer announced they would be taking a break, and Clint turned his head and watched them walk off stage. In doing so, something in the hand of one of the men at the next table caught his attention. He had a gold coin in his hand and was rolling it up and down through his fingers. The coin looked familiar.

"Excuse me for a second," he said to Shayla and walked over the man. "Could I see that coin for a second?"

The man looked up at him, and the conversation at the table stopped. The man with the coin had jet black hair and Clint's first impression was that he might be a native Alaskan, an Eskimo. "No, go away."

"If you don't mind," Clint said and stretched his hand out, palm up, so the man might put the coin in it.

Instead, the man stood up and put the coin in his pocket.

All four of the other men stood up, and the one closest to Clint pulled at Clint's shoulder, trying to back him away.

"I don't mean any trouble. It's just I'm a collector." The other four men all had on overalls, working clothes. The man with the coin was dressed similar to Clint in jeans and a dark tee shirt.

"Get lost," he said again, and the man behind Clint pulled at his shoulder again.

Clint brushed the hand off his shoulder and would have stepped away, but the man who had his hand on Clint jumped him and tried to throw him to the floor. Clint spun out of the man's grip, breaking the man's little finger in the process. The man's scream when the finger snapped brought all four of the men into the fray, attacking Clint in unison. In the movies, they come at you one at a time, giving the protagonist time to show off his or her excellent fighting skills. In real life this is a luxury that rarely happens. The bad guys come at you in a pack.

Still, Clint, using every nasty trick in the book, made good headway against the group until someone hit him on the back of his head with something that felt like a brick and sent him sprawling to the floor. The room started spinning, and Clint had the sensation he was passing out when someone kicked him in the ribs. The pain from the kick kept him from passing out but did nothing to stop the room from spinning. Although his mind lacked focus, he thought the men walked away from him.

"Clint, Clint, we need to go," Shayla said. She tried to pick him up off the floor. A man from another table came over and helped get Clint into a sitting position.

"If you can, you need to take him out the back door. Those

guys only left because they thought they may have killed him. If they see you walk out the front door, or if they come back in, they may try to finish the job," the man said.

Clint heard their voices but had a hard time focusing on what was being said. "Can you get up?" the man asked.

Shayla pulled at Clint's arm, and the man gripped his other arm. Between the two of them and a little help from Clint, they got him standing.

"Here, give him a sip of this," their server stuck a shot glass in front of Clint's face. Shayla took it from her and tilted it into Clint's mouth.

The cheap whiskey burned going down and made Clint gag, but it also brought him back into the world of the living. He immediately put his hand to his head. The man who had been holding the arm stepped away.

"Are you okay," he asked.

"Damn, what hit me?" Clint said and leaned on Shayla as the room tried to start spinning again.

"It was like one of those blackjacks the police used to use. The skinny guy had it and hit you while your back was to him. It was a cheap shot, and he hit you hard. You better go," the man who had helped him up said.

"If you can walk out of here, you should leave now," said another man who had walked up.

Clint resented being told what to do, but Shayla tugged at him, and he wasn't sure he could remain standing there without her support. He followed her out the back door.

"My place is just down the road," she said.

They didn't walk far, but twice Shayla had to plead with him to keep walking and stay awake. When Clint's mind finally became clear, he found himself sitting on a recliner in a small apartment. His head throbbed with pain and his mouth felt dry. Shayla was in the process of putting a blanket over him.

"Thanks. Guess I kind of ruined our evening."

She looked at him funny. "I guess they did scramble your brains, but thanks for saying that."

"Who were those guys?"

"People you should never have messed with. They are not nice men. I should have warned you, but you went to their table before I could say anything. They work at the old fishery about three miles down the coast line. I recognized three of them, maybe one of the other two. They're asses. I try to stay away from them, and you should, too."

"I will in the future."

"Why'd you go over there and bother them anyway?"

"What?" For a second, Clint couldn't think of a reason, then it all came back. The coin. He almost said it was nothing, but thought she might have knowledge that could help. "The gold coin the one guy had. He kept rolling it up and down his fingers in his right hand. Did you notice it?"

"I saw it."

"I just asked him if I could see it, and they went crazy."

"I told you they aren't nice. They would drive in the wrong lane if they could hit a dog. Then they would laugh about it."

"Have you seen other gold coins like that around here?"

"No. The whole history around here is based on the old gold rush days, but those days are over. Now it's just the tourism that keeps this place alive."

"Any gold stores?"

"Tourist stores, but there is a place you can bring in any gold you do find, if you find any, when you go prospecting. That's not coins though," Shayla said. "Tourists go out panning for gold, but that's just for fun. Can I get you a drink or anything?"

"No, thank you. Why didn't anyone call the police or an ambulance back there?"

"Not worth it over a fight, especially if no one dies. A lot of fighting goes on up here, especially in the winter. All these men thinking they're the toughest man in town. When they get in groups, they can be more dangerous."

The pack mentality, Clint understood it well. People do many things to go along with the gang or group that they would never do on their own.

"This fish processing place where these men work, could an airplane land out there?" Clint asked.

"Of course. There's a little inlet there where a plane could land when the water is smooth enough. They have a dock and everything. It's much easier to do things from the inlets and rivers around here than the sea. There are other fishing camps all up and down here, too."

Clint thought about the possibilities. There weren't many here, but at least this one had some potential. A place a plane could land, the coin, and a group of bad men with whom he'd like to settle a score.

Shayla started unbuttoning her blouse. "You feel like spending some time with me?"

"Shayla, I'd like to, but my head is still killing me. I'm afraid I'm more likely to throw up than anything else right now."

"I'm sorry, and I understand. Anyway, could I borrow a

few dollars from you? My rent is due, and I don't want to go back out there tonight. I'll owe you."

"What do you need?"

"Fifty?"

Clint pulled three twenties out of his wallet. "Here. I may need your help again."

"Thank you. Anything you want, anytime."

"For now, can you just walk me out and point me in the direction of the Pacific Vistas Bed and Breakfast."

CHAPTER 31

Other than sore ribs and a very tender bump on the head, Clint felt surprisingly fine the next morning. He had slept in more than usual, and he felt his body needed it. Downstairs, he settled for two large cups of coffee and two cinnamon cake donuts for breakfast, despite the managers' push to have him eat more.

"Is it possible to rent a boat to sightsee up and down the coastline?"

The manager, who worked both the front desk and the adjacent dining room, had to be around sixty. He had a perfect, large, circular bald spot on the top of his head surrounded by thin grey, almost whitish hair. He also had a smile that never seemed to leave his face,

"You can rent most anything here. Harder to buy something. Must be thirty men and women who would take you anywhere for a fee. If you're a fisherman, which I guess you aren't, there are dozens of great spots along the coast near here where the fishing is great."

"Would I find them hanging around the docks?"

"That's where I'd look," the old man grinned and rubbed his chin. "Old Mary might be the most reliable and cheapest."

"Is that the name of the boat or the person?"

"Ha! Good one, name of the captain. She ain't actually that old, but that's what everyone calls her."

The manager wondered over to a young couple that entered the dining room. He helped them to a table and brought them both water and what Clint thought was hot chocolate. A minute later the manager returned to Clint and sat down at his table. "Do you mind?"

"Not at all."

"Young honeymooners. Wish I was their age again," he said.

Clint smiled and took the last bite of his second donut.

"If you use Old Mary, she's usually on her boat by ten each day. Tell her old Mike Shine sent you. May get you a discount."

"Well thank you, Mike, I'll do that."

"Mike is not really my name. It's Mark, but she'll know. Uh oh, here's more customers," Mark said and went to greet them.

Clint finished his coffee and went back to his room to get his jacket. On the way to the docks, he bought binoculars and a black stocking cap. He considered buying a heavier jacket, but decided the one he had would do. A steady wind blew in off the sea, and Clint knew it might be chilly out over the water.

The walk to the harbor area only took about ten minutes. The place seemed busier than the late afternoon on the day before. He checked his phone and didn't see any messages, but it did tell him the time, ten minutes past ten.

Finding Old Mary wasn't difficult, but his walking up and down the pier brought him a lot of stares from various men and women who likely wondered what he was doing checking them all out.

He stopped at an old boat that had seen better days. A woman stood on the deck and sprayed water along the stern. Clint saw pieces of what he thought was fish falling off into the water below. She looked at him. Clint had always wondered why some women were referred to as handsome, an adjective he thought best used with men, but that word came to mind as soon as she looked at him.

She had on tan overalls, black rubber boots, and a long sleeve navy blue pullover. Her light brown hair had touches of grey and was mostly pulled back tight, except for a few pieces that had apparently escaped and hung free around her face.

"What are you staring at?" she asked.

"Are you Mary?"

"Depends. Are you from a collection agency or the IRS?"

"No, just looking for a boat to rent and Mike Shine said to ask for Old Mary," Clint said and grinned.

"God, Mark won't ever let me live that one down. One drunken night in the back of his parent's Subaru, and he can't get over the fact that I didn't even know his name. Kept calling him Mike all night. Hell, I wouldn't even remember the night, if it wasn't for the name screwup."

Clint didn't detect any animosity in her voice, and she seemed in a good mood.

"When would you need a boat?"

"The sooner the better."

"Fishing?"

"No, just sightseeing."

"How about this morning then. My day is free. Are you by yourself?" Mary asked.

"Yes."

"I can be ready in about fifteen minutes. If you need to run and get anything, do it now."

"Don't need anything," Clint said.

She studied him for a few seconds. "Where do you want to go?"

"Just want to do some observing of the coastline and some of the inlets south of here."

"How far south?"

"Only a few miles, although I'm not sure."

"Some of the inlets go in for several miles themselves."

"How much would it cost me for the whole day?"

Mary smiled. "You a beer drinker? There's a fridge down the stairs, make yourself at home. Oh, and by the way, you passed at least four security cameras getting to my boat. If that concerns you in any way, you might want to reconsider what you're doing here."

"Not concerned at all," Clint said and went down into the cabin below. The boat had the typical upper station that housed the pilot or captain's position for operating the boat, and a cabin below deck that looked like one medium size room, until Clint found a narrow door that led into a small lavatory.

He looked into the refrigerator and selected a Gatorade. With the price she was charging, he figured he owned everything in the fridge. He felt warmer in the cabin than up in the breeze off the water, so he sat down and looked at one of the fishing magazines piled on a small coffee table. He noticed the table was bolted to the floor.

After a few minutes, Mary yelled from the deck above for him to come up. He did and found her up at the controls for the boat. "Come on up here for a minute," she said. "There's two seats up here, besides I need to collect payment before we leave."

Clint paid by credit card, and while she processed the payment through a small attachment on her phone, he studied the boat's control panel with all its screens and dials.

"Don't worry we have a fairly modern system here. Weather," she pointed to one of the screens. Shows us any storms around us. "Both marine radio and satellite phone capabilities. And over here, radar, so we can see what other ships are in the area. We also can tell the depth of the water we're in, and a few more boring things, like oil pressure and fuel levels. Just want you to know we should be safe out there, but in case something does happen, we have life vests scattered all around in plain sight, and even a small, inflatable raft."

"How cold is the water around here?"

"Too cold to go swimming, but some do. We won't be getting far from shore, and if anything does happen, the first thing I'll do is steer us toward land."

"Sounds fair," Clint said.

"You ready?"

"Yes. Are you the only crew?"

"Usually Terrence is with me, but this week he went to Anchorage to visit his folks. If all you want to do is sightsee, we don't need anyone else.

Mary backed the boat away from the dock and slowly steered it out into the open water before accelerating to what Clint guessed was the boat's cruising speed. The wind built up to the point where Clint regretted not getting a heavier coat.

"A bit chilly out here over the water, isn't it?" Mary said.

"Yes, but not bad up here out of the wind."

"Well, we have a couple of things to help us out." She turned a knob and warm air immediately began blowing out of a vent by his feet. "Helps a little up here, but with the back open, it doesn't do much when it gets really cold."

"Can you close off the back?"

"I have a plastic cover I can snap on, but it's more effective against rain than the cold. I rarely use it, because it's a pain to put up and take down - not to mention storing it. It won't be bad today anyway."

"I didn't mean for today, I was just curious," Clint said "What was the second thing you said you had to fight the cold?"

"Hot coffee, let me know if you want some."

"I will. You get a much better perspective of the mountains out here looking back at Skagway." Clint went down the few steps and stood along the port side of the boat. He estimated the boat measured forty feet in length. It handled the swells and waves well, but didn't think it would survive in any real weather. Taking the binoculars out of the bag he was still carrying, he looked back at Skagway. He saw a woman standing against the perimeter fence around the docks. She looked like Shayla.

The boat turned parallel to the coast about a half mile off shore. Clint wondered why he didn't see anyone fishing either from shore or in boats closer to the shore. As they slowly moved away from Skagway, he understood why everyone had told him that not many people live outside Skagway. It looked like rough country. A few nice cabins and houses could be seen along the shoreline near Skagway, nestled back in the trees, and with boats docked in an adjacent small inlet. However, these houses became rare as the boat moved farther away from the small city.

"Those binoculars look like some I got when I was a teenager. If you want to use some good ones, they're up there," Mary motioned up to where she had been.

"Boat driving itself?"

She smiled. "We have all sorts of modern things on this old bird. It'll go straight, but I don't ever leave it for more than a minute or two. Come back up and tell me exactly what you're looking for, so I can do a better job getting you where you want to go. First, though, I'm going down to get some coffee. Want some?"

"I'll have a cup, black."

"Coming right up." She disappeared down below, and Clint focused his attention back on the shoreline. The view was beautiful, an outdoorsman's paradise. Now alone, he began thinking how much he should tell Mary about why he was really there.

CHAPTER 32

Mary returned with a thermos of coffee and motioned for him to join her up in the pilot's station. When he got there, she had two cups on the counter into which she was pouring coffee. He took one and thanked her, noticing that she also drank her coffee black.

"Listen, I can get closer to the shore whenever you want, and there's a couple places close by where we can go in some coves, inlets, a river, you have it. But it would be nice if you'd be a little more specific."

"Alright, but please keep what I tell you to yourself. "

"Don't be so dramatic. Who would I tell? It's not like I have a lot of people in my life right now."

"It's not that. I'm here looking for someone who disappeared. If word got out, she could be harmed."

"Wife? Girlfriend? Or are you a private investigator?"

"Not a wife, maybe an exaggerated mixture of the latter two if I was being honest."

Mary smiled. "You know, even if she's here, maybe she came here voluntarily. Maybe she needed space from you."

"If that was the case, I never would've come. No, I have it on very good authority she didn't come on her own free will."

"You know it's beautiful country, and I love it up here, but Skagway only has a couple thousand residents and there aren't but a handful that actually live out there away from town." Mary nodded at the shoreline. "It's kind of crazy to think she ended up out there. I've known most of the residents in and around the city for years. The word would get out if some new person moved in with any of them. Gossip is a fine art up here, as is spying on your neighbor. Hell, like I said, most of them are related to each other."

"That should actually make my job easier."

"So, you think someone, what, kidnapped her and brought her here? Here? That's about as illogical as can be. And from where? You can't easily get here from the forty-eight."

"Believe me, I know how hard it is to get here. But someone could land a plane on the water and not be observed, right?"

"Yes, and someone could come by boat and not be observed. Look over there," Mary pointed toward a section on the coastline that bent into the land before coming back out. That's a cove, not a very big one, but it twists around in there, and there's a nice house back in there with a very nice dock. Nice people there, can't see them involved."

"I hear there's a fishery down this way."

"The main fishery is back in the city. There's an old one a couple more miles down the coast. They do some business, cause I've seen a couple fishing boats go in and out there, but I think it's barely staying afloat."

"Been there?"

"No, and I'm not taking you there. You'd better hope your lady friend is not there."

"Why?"

"Those men are nasty. I've heard too many stories. The law has been out there a few times, too, but can't ever pin anything on those guys. The guy that runs it is a big man, well over six feet tall and heavy set. He supposedly killed another man several years back. Witnesses said it was self-defense, of course all the witnesses worked for him."

"Could a plane land by the fishery?"

"Yes, but were you listening? We're not going there."

"How close will you take me?"

Mary mumbled something just loud enough to remind Clint that she was a sailor.

"Thanks." Clint knew it was a long shot, but it was the only shot he had. If he hadn't seen the coin, he wouldn't have asked Mary to take him down here. He didn't get a close enough look at the coin to see if it was like his, but from what he did see, it sure looked like the ones he had found, and the only one unaccounted for was in Forthsyte's possession when he was murdered.

When Mary finally turned the boat towards shore, Clint thought they had come a lot further than the three miles Shayla had mentioned. Of course, why would she know the exact distance?

"Is this a river?" Clint asked as they entered what looked like the wide mouth of a river that flowed into the sea.

"No, the coastline just formed this way. Like part of the glacier cut through here before receding back. This whole body of water around Skagway and up to Haines is like a fjord. None of it is very wide, but its deep."

"Am I wrong calling it a sea?"

"Not to me."

"Where's the fishery?"

"Not too far." Mary slowed the boat. "I'll be right back." She disappeared down to the cabin below. Clint thought she needed to use the bathroom, but she returned in seconds fastening a holster around her waist. A large revolver fit snugly into it.

"Don't worry, I won't ask you to take me close enough to use that thing."

"I wouldn't go there if you did. This is in case they send a boat out to see what we're doing. I've been threatened by them before."

"The authorities let them get away with that?"

"They've been visited by the state police and the fish and wildlife people before and told to cool it."

"Have they actually hurt anyone? I mean other than that one man in a fight."

"None that they can prove," something in Mary's look made Clint wonder. "People have disappeared around here, and there are rumors. I just don't like or trust them."

"There it is," Mary said, pointing at a couple of warehouse-looking buildings next to three smaller ones.

Clint looked at the complex through his binoculars and saw a fishing boat, three times the size of Mary's, docked near the buildings. People were carrying things off the boat and into one of the warehouses.

"That's good. They'll likely be too busy to worry about us," Mary said. "I'm still going to keep us a couple hundred yards offshore and turn around as we get even with it."

"What do they do with the fish that is brought in there?"

"Process it." She looked at him like he wasn't very bright.

"I mean do they can it, smoke it, freeze it?"

"I don't know. It may look right now like they are very busy, but from what I understand, they do very little business in the area. I don't think they have their own brand. Some large company owns it. The product gets intermingled with that of other small suppliers, and I assume ends up in grocery markets throughout Canada and the U.S., maybe even overseas."

"And they have another boat like that one?"

"Yes, I'm sure of that. They're in and out of the harbor in Skagway, but I don't believe they own the boats. Most likely, the crew and boats are contracted with them."

"What have the crew said about the people that run that place?" Clint looked at the fishery as he spoke.

"They pay well, but don't talk much about their operations. I mean that's what the crew says about the people at the fishery. The boats, now that I think more about it, I'm sure aren't owned by the fishery. The two have separate long term contracts."

Mary started turning the boat, while Clint tried to see anything that might supply him with a clue that Frankie could be there. "Here, use these, and you can tell the time off their watches." She handed him her large binoculars.

"I see what you mean," Clint said, as he studied the people coming in and out of what he guessed was the main building. He saw two men whom he remembered from the jazz club. They were supervising the offloading. As he watched, he got the feeling that more than supervising, they were ensuring that no one drifted off to some other building in the complex.

"Are the guys on the fishing boats as bad as the ones at the fishery?"

"No, not at all. Don't get me wrong, half these guys will fight you for just looking at them wrong, but most of them are good, hard working guys. May be a few women in the crew, too. They'd fight you, too," Mary said and laughed. "Got to be tough up here."

"Where do they go from here?"

"Anywhere, although they often take advantage of

Skagway while they're this close."

"Think any of them might talk to me?" Clint asked.

"Depends, but maybe not. They'll think you're just snooping, and that won't motivate them to talk to you. Besides, I doubt if they've seen anything more than what they see when they offload and onload their boat."

Clint continued watching the activity on shore.

"You really think she might be there?"

"I have no idea, just some weak evidence that she may have been brought here by plane a few days ago." Maybe a week, he thought.

"Okay, I'll tell you what I'll do, but no promises. If this crew spends the night in Skagway, and I can get one of them out to dinner, I'll let you know, and you can join us. You're buying and no rough stuff."

"Thanks."

"I'm only doing this out of pity and mostly in case there is a woman held prisoner in there. Unless someone has seen her, the law isn't going to go looking for her."

"I know. It's a long shot. Let me ask you one more thing. What's your schedule like the next couple of days?"

"Depends, I'm not doing anything foolish."

"Don't worry, Mary, I'll be the one doing the foolish things."

She didn't say anything for a few seconds. "I'm busy tomorrow until early afternoon. I'm free the day after tomorrow. Like I said, my crewman is out of town, so I'm not doing any fishing charters."

"Do you mind being out after dark?"

"Not if the weather is good, and it should be all week."

"Thanks. What I'd like to do is have you drop me off along the shore a mile from the fishery. I'd like to check it out a little more closely."

"You're crazy, you know. It's dark in those woods, and the ground is anything but flat. If you reach the fishery without breaking your leg, I'm sure they have a fence around it. They may even have dogs. Besides, you think she'll be outside?"

"I know, but will you help?"

"Cost will be double."

"I'll pay you triple," Clint said. "I may need to go back out a second night."

"For triple, I'll take you there all week." Mary grinned when she said this, and Clint wondered if he might need her to.

CHAPTER 33

Dinner that night never happened as the fishing boat didn't come to Skagway.

"I told you it wasn't a sure thing," Mary said over the phone.

"I know," Clint said, "I'd still like for you to take me back tomorrow."

"I've got you written down, don't worry."

"One more thing, what's the name of the fishery? I don't remember seeing a name on any of the buildings while we were out there."

"It used to be called C.H. Fishery, but don't know if it still goes by that name, but the same guy has been running it for years."

"Know his name?"

"I've heard him referred to as Chappie but nothing more," Mary said. "Be careful who you ask about him, and for God's sake, don't mention me if you do."

"I won't. See you tomorrow."

Clint spent the evening trying to learn a little more about Chappie and C.H. Fishery. He asked Eric at Rudolph's over dinner.

"The fishery south of here? Didn't think it was still open. I mean, I guess I knew they still had a couple people working down there, but I haven't seen anything sold around here with their name on it."

"How about this Chappie guy who runs it?" Clint asked.

"You learn up here not to ask about people. Stick to your

own business. It can be a long, dangerous winter."

"No comment, then?"

"No, except stay away from him. I, for one, would rather slap a bear than mess with him. Now that's enough talk." Eric walked away and despite the lack of other customers did not come back to talk to Clint.

Later that evening over a beer at the small bar inside the Pacific Vistas, Clint asked Mark about Chappie.

"That man has been bad news forever and worse for anyone who messes with him. So, the good news is that I don't know him well enough to say anything about him."

"Anything?"

"Nope, and I wouldn't be asking people in town about him. The most you can hope for is for them to ignore you, the worse is they would get word back to him. You seem like a good guy, Clint. I don't know what your interest is with him, but let it go."

Clint sipped on his beer and thought it might be better to keep his presence in Skagway a surprise. He decided to change the topic.

"Mary remembered you."

Mark beamed. "She's always been a character, and a bit of a wild one, too. I must have been close to thirty, still living with my parents, fast tracking it to loser status. Why she hooked up with me that one night still amazes me. I doubt if she was twenty at the time, but kids grow up fast up here"

"Did you two have a relationship after that?"

"Ha, no, but I look at that as a turning point in my life. I thought she didn't want to go out with me, because I still lived at home. I got a real job, a place of my own, and started taking care of myself. I never could get Mary back, but I found my wife and a new life."

"Things turned out alright, then."

"Yes, yes they did."

When Clint returned to his room, he sent a text to Buzz. "What can you tell me about a C.H. Fishery near Skagway and a man called Chappie who runs it?" He knew he wouldn't hear anything right away.

The next morning, he was up and dressed early, taking a Styrofoam cup of coffee with him for a walk around the town. The brisk air felt good, and the sky for once was cloudless. He wondered if the weather was a good omen or a trick, like being dealt two quick fours only to sucker you into a hand that never gets any better. Been there, done that, he thought.

The streets were empty this early which suited Clint fine. He entered the store where he had earlier purchased the binoculars.

"We're not really open yet, but if you know what you want, I'll be glad to help you," said a teenager who walked up to him as he entered.

"Do you have any night vision equipment?" Clint asked.

"Sure. Cameras or goggles?"

"May I see both?"

"Come over here, and like I said, and I don't mean to be rude, we're not open to browsing."

Clint grinned and followed the kid to a corner of the store that displayed a small assortment of night vision equipment. He recognized the brand and make of the goggles, thinking they would be sufficient for his needs. "I'll buy those and how about the smallest camera that you have. Like that one." He pointed into a glass cabinet.

Leaving the store, Clint imagined he could have purchased

the same equipment online for a third of what they charged him. He doubted Section would care, but if they did, he would use his own money to pay for the equipment. Rather than finish his walk, Clint decided to head back to the Pacific Vistas to check out his new purchases and have breakfast.

"What do you have there?" Mark asked. He was in the back when Clint went through the small buffet, grabbing a pile of bacon, eggs, and toast.

"Some night vision stuff. Thought I'd go out tonight and see if I can see some of the wildlife around here."

"Don't really need to go out at night. You can see them during the day. Although, I guess the wolves only come out at night, and it's best not to get so close you can see them."

"Wolves? Are you serious?"

"Yes. Some have been seen at the dump at dusk. Mostly bear you need to watch out for. They're more common, and don't believe that nonsense they won't bother you. They'll do whatever they want to do, and if that includes taking a bite out of you, they will."

"Thanks for the reassurance."

Mark smiled. "The life you save may be your own."

"I think that has to do with Smokey the Bear."

"You can't expect for me to know the names of the bears around here. Have you used that stuff before?"

"Yes," Clint said, "while I was in the military. Not this brand but similar equipment. I just need to read the brochures to get a little smarter with them."

"Well, I'll leave you to it," Mark said and walked over to inspect the buffet line.

CHAPTER 34

The text from Buzz came in about fifteen minutes before Clint was going to head down to the docks. "First glance at the fishery revealed nothing of interest. Profitable business the last few years with sales about five million dollars. Can't find any mention of a Chappie on the company's filings on record. For what it's worth, we have found some evidence that a plane may have flown in and out of there, or near there, around the same time the boss thinks Frankie may have been taken there. Be careful."

One more reason to check the place out, he thought. Too bad they didn't come up with any information on Chappie, but it made sense if Chappie was a nickname.

Just before six, Clint arrived at the docks and joined Mary on her boat.

"Still want to do this?" Mary asked.

"Yes, I'll just be looking not touching."

"Then we should go. I'd like to get you onshore before it gets too dark. Easier for you to get around and easier for me to get you where you want to go. You got everything you need?" She asked eyeing his backpack.

"I'm ready," Clint said.

After a few minutes of untethering the boat and other preparations, Mary steered the boat away from the harbor. "When we get there, I'll take you onshore in the run-about, lock in the GPS coordinates, come back towards Skagway a half mile or so, and wait. When you're done, I'll come back and get you. How long are you going to need?"

"How far away from the place are you dropping me off?"

"I'd rather not turn into the inlet, so maybe a mile. They shouldn't hear us or see us, and as I won't be lingering near the mouth no one passing by should notice."

"Three hours should be enough."

"It should be," Mary said. "The terrain will be rough, but you should be able to reach the compound in an hour. That gives you an hour to look around, although I still don't know what you expect to see. You know you can check it out on Google Earth."

"Already have, but it's the little things that can screw things up."

"I'm not even going to ask what you mean by that."

Clint grinned at her, "I just want to be careful. May I have a cup of your coffee?"

"Have all you want. You've more than paid for it."

They reached the drop off spot quicker than Clint expected. "Get yourself ready. I don't want to linger here."

"I came ready."

A small electric winch made getting the small craft overboard and into the water easy, and in less than five minutes they were on their way to shore. The rocky shoreline forced them to take a few minutes to find an ideal spot to bring the raft up to dry land.

"Make a note of this spot's GPS on your phone. I'll do the same. I don't want to be sailing around looking for you," Mary said.

"Will do. See you in three hours," Clint said.

Mary nodded and steered the boat away from shore. Clint

moved into the trees but stopped to watch Mary successfully get back onto her boat. He recorded the GPS location and the timer on his phone for three hours. While he also had the GPS setting for the fishery, he didn't plan on using it. He would stay just inside the tree line and follow the shore around to it.

Enough daylight remained that he thought he could make good time getting to the fishery, but he knew it would be slower coming back in the dark. He removed his Beretta and a shoulder holster from his backpack. He didn't know how bad the terrain would get and wanted the weapon snug against him with little chance of being bumped out. He put his jacket back on and wondered if he should have brought gloves. The sun had set, and the air off the water seemed to be getting cooler.

Clint started moving and quickly realized his travel wouldn't be as fast as he thought. Flat terrain seemed to be the exception rather than the norm. Even staying close to the shore, he had to clamor over numerous rocky ridges. Twice he had to go right out the water's edge to get past a steep fifteen to twenty foot of sheer rock. Although he kept an eye out for any form of wildlife to include other humans, he didn't see anything during his trek other than birds.

By the time he reached a point where he could clearly see the fishery, the last bit of daylight disappeared from the sky. He removed his night vision goggles and camera from his backpack and studied the fishery. He didn't see any sign of life. He took a couple of photos before moving away from the water. Every fifty yards or so repeated the process, taking a few pictures. A few times the tree line allowed him to get within twenty yards of the compound and even closer to the fence, giving him a good angle to take pictures.

An eight-foot tall, chain link fence surrounded the fishery. He saw two gates padlocked shut and took pictures of them. His trip to the far side of the fishery served to give him a feel for the place but little else. When he turned around to retrace his steps back, he studied the compound for ways to get in and back out. The place had a few outdoor lights on poles but none of them were turned on or perhaps no longer worked. He didn't see any guards, but why would they need them here?

He had only come about a third of the way around the fishery and had stopped to take a couple more pictures of one of the gates, when he heard a voice.

"Time to get back inside. Come on, now!" a man barked.

The light from a door being open broke the darkness and for a brief moment blinded him. Luckily the light wasn't that bright and didn't shine directly out towards him. He removed his goggles and grabbed the binoculars. Looking back at the doorway, he was in time to see the backs of two people enter through it and the door closing behind them. He thought the two were men because of their short hair, but something tugged in the back of his mind.

He continued to the water's edge and looked back at the compound one last time, before turning and making his way back to the rendezvous point. About half way back, he sensed something or someone following him. Three times he stopped and listened. He considered getting his night vision goggles out of his backpack, but each time he stopped he couldn't hear anything. Enough of the moon had appeared over the mountains to provide a little light. Not much but enough that Clint thought he would see movement.

On his last stop, he waited a full minute before moving on.

The wind had picked up and Clint decided the sounds he heard may have come from the wind rustling through the forest around him.

"Well, was it worth it?" Mary asked after they secured the smaller craft onto her boat.

"Yes. Had to do it either way."

"Still want to come back tomorrow?

"I think so. I'll let you know if I want to cancel."

"You could ask the authorities for help," she said.

"I don't have enough evidence for them to do anything but maybe talk to them, and that's not something that will help the situation."

"It's your life, you can lose it in any way you choose."

"Thanks," he said and meant it.

Mary kept looking around on their journey to Skagway.

"Nervous?" Clint asked.

"Damn straight." She didn't elaborate, and Clint didn't ask.

After they tied up at the dock, Clint said, "Tomorrow, I'd like to leave about this time. Is that going to be a problem?"

"No."

"Okay, I'll be in touch," Clint said and walked into town, leaving Mary to finish whatever she needed to do on her boat.

He wondered why she was sticking her neck out for him. The extra money may have motivated her to help, but still, she had to know there would be a risk to her, too. If he failed tomorrow night, and they discovered she had helped him, she would be in danger. She had to have her reasons, he thought, and wondered if he needed to know what they were before he got off her boat tomorrow night for his attempt to rescue Frankie.

Back in his room, he transferred the pictures he had taken of the fishery to his laptop with the hope that the larger screen would make it easier to study all the details in the photos. He wanted to go directly to the pictures he took right before he heard the man and saw the two people, but he forced himself to go through them in order, retracing his movements as they took place. In doing so, he surprised himself when he saw a person sitting in the dark in a photo he took during his outward trek around the perimeter. He hadn't noticed the person when he took the picture.

He zoomed in on the person and did everything he could to enhance the clarity of the photo. The person was alone and had both elbows on his legs and hands pressing against both sides of his face. The face was tilted downward. But was it a man? The hair was cut short like a man's, but something about the person nagged at Clint.

He checked the photo before and after the one with the person, but neither covered the same spot and no one else could be seen. He continued through the photos and stopped when he came back to the spot on his return from the far side of the compound. Unfortunately, he had no pictures of the exact spot. He recalled that he was looking through his goggles when he heard the voice and saw the people. He went immediately to the binoculars to get a better look, not the camera.

He focused on the vision in his mind of the two people walking into the building. One was taller than the other. He thought they were men because of their haircuts, and one of them spoke with a male voice, but what about the other? One person had on a lightweight jacket and some form of pants. The other was wearing what looked like a robe.

"Dammit!" he said aloud. A thought came to mind that Buzz might be able to enhance the one photo that he had of the person sitting in the dark. He attached it to a text and sent it to Buzz. He knew it would still be early morning there and that Buzz was likely not yet awake, so he didn't expect a quick reply.

He took a shower and despite his recent escapade in the woods, went to sleep after a few minutes of tossing and turning in bed.

CHAPTER 35

Shayla surprised him as he walked out of the Pacific Vistas the next morning. "Clint," she called for him from the side of the building. She approached him when he turned to look at her. "I need to tell you something." She looked around as though she thought someone might be watching her.

"Are you okay?" Clint asked. A reddish-blue swelling nearly closed her left eye.

"I wanted to warn you. The men you got into a fight with want to finish their fight with you. I didn't tell them where you were staying and only told them your first name."

"Did they do this to you?"

"One of them, but I'll be fine. He said he wanted to know where he could find you, because you hurt his friend, and he said the guys wanted to finish the job, to put you in the ground. That's what he said."

"He hit you?"

"Yes, and it scared me, but I made it sound good that I didn't know anything more. I asked him why he thought I would know the life story of every john in my life. That's the truth ninety percent of the time anyway. It was easy to lie, and then I just had to distract him, which I found disgusting, but he left me alone after he was done."

"You think that was it? He was just looking for me because they want to finish the fight somewhere where they won't be distracted by an audience?"

"Yes. I'm sure of it. He said no one gets away with hurting

one of his guys."

"Who was this guy?"

"Don't go looking for him. They'll kill you and hurt me more."

"Was it a guy called Chappie?" Clint asked.

Shayla's eyes opened wide. "Thank god, no. Do you know him? Never go near him."

"Why do you say that?"

Shayla shook her head but didn't respond. She took a step backward.

"Hey," Clint said. "I won't ask any more questions, and if I see any of those men in Skagway, I'll steer clear of them."

"Good, and I can't be seen with you anymore. I took a chance coming here. If you want me, come to my place after dark. Please be careful. You're a nice man." She turned and almost ran away.

Clint watched her for a few seconds and decided to give her a bit of space and time before he started walking into town. He returned inside the Pacific Vistas and poured a cup of coffee.

"What was that all about, if you don't mind my asking?" Mark Shine asked.

"Nothing," Clint said.

"Was she bothering you? I mean do you know her?"

"I've met her, but if you mean am I a customer, the answer is no."

"Sorry, none of my business, but I saw her accost you outside. I've known her for years, and I feel a little sorry for her, but I don't want that kind of behavior, you know, around my place."

"I understand, and I doubt she'll be back," Clint said. He

finished the coffee and left.

Less than a minute later, his phone vibrated with a text. "Call me when you get a chance – Buzz"

He stopped walking and started to make the call from the street when he noticed a coffee shop a few steps away. The Northern Grind looked like it had recently opened, and two energetic young men were bouncing between taking orders, serving the coffee, and chatting up the three customers. Clint thought they may have already had one too many expressos. Clint sat down at one of the two small tables in the coffee shop.

"You need to order at the counter, sir," one of the men said to him from behind the counter. The three customers were bunched together at the end of the counter, having already gotten their orders. They laughed loudly about something, and Clint wondered if he should've stayed on the street to make the call. He had already had a couple cups of coffee that morning. However, he was there and the place likely needed the business to survive, so he went to the counter and ordered a cappuccino.

"I'll bring it to you when it's ready," the barista said.

Clint returned to his table and was happily surprised when the three noisy customers left as he sat down. He called Buzz.

"What's up?"

"It's her, Clint. Her hair's been cut short and there's some swelling to the left side of her face, but it's her."

Clint wanted to end the call and head straight out to the fishery. It took him a second to realize Buzz had started talking again.

"….. been discussing how to handle this –"

Clint cut him off. "Buzz, I'm going in after her. You try to bring the authorities in on this, and they'll kill her and whoever else they may have there and get rid of the bodies before the cops could ever get access."

"Hold on, Clint, let me finish. The boss, Dolly, and I all agree with you. The last time the authorities tried raiding those guys they got massacred. They'll want to do it, but they will argue and disagree as to how and when. They'll also want to be sure of what they're doing. They can't afford a repeat of what happened outside Anchorage. Any advance signal to these guys that they are about to be raided, and we also believe they will get rid of anything and everything incriminating."

Clint had a little trouble following who these guys and those guys were, but he got the gist and agreed with Buzz.

"I'm going in tonight."

"We figured that."

"Only two people here have any idea what I'm doing, and maybe that's really just one. They believe this is just personal, which in a way is true."

"That's the way it's got to be, Clint. We can't send in help. If something happens to you everything dies with you, unless the local press or authorities get involved. In that case, we stay out of the picture other than leaking that you were searching for a missing woman, and then only if they can't discover that on their own."

"That's fine."

"Something else, we dug deeper into the international conglomerate that is the parent company for the fishery. Through another, separate holding company, the international conglomerate also owns the same shell company that was buying up the properties next to our military installations. We're keeping that to ourselves now, but at some point, weeks from now, we will share that information with the intel community. We need to separate ourselves from whatever happens tonight."

"Makes sense to me."

"One more thing, Clint. Deer believes that if you do succeed tonight, they will make an all-out effort to stop Frankie or you from talking to anyone. They must have some sort of support infrastructure in Skagway, so it would be best if you got her out of there straight away."

"I've thought about that, but she won't have a passport or even a driver's license to get her into Canada or for that matter onto an airplane. We could catch a ferry to Juneau but that will make us a slow-moving easy target."

"No, car is the best bet. You're only a few minutes away from the border, and you'll have a passport for her this afternoon. One was already made up for her, and after seeing the photo this morning, we sent it out. Deer has a connection with a private charter outfit that owes her a big favor, plus we're a good customer."

Clint grinned, "I'm impressed again."

"You should be, now just don't screw up your part. I enjoy our little talks, and Dolly would be heartbroken."

"I'll be okay, and I'll stay in touch. Anything else? I have a few things to do."

"No, good luck."

The call ended, and Clint grinned again. Up until the call with Buzz, he hadn't solved the matter of getting Frankie out of Skagway. He had made a mental list of everything he could do to be prepared, but getting her out of town did not have a solution. He thought she might be too big to fit in his trunk, but had considered that his last resort.

He purchased a handful of items in town that he thought they would need for their trip out of Alaska, topped off the gas in his car, and paid his room bill through another night. He had already located a spot to park his car close to the harbor but not in any of the designated harbor parking lots.

Returning to his room for a long afternoon nap, he received a text from Section with a link to a picture of the blueprints to the fishery. A note said they might be outdated, but Clint studied them in detail before getting into bed. It would be a long night, and he needed to be rested before it began.

His alarm woke him at seven.

CHAPTER 36

Mary had the boat prepared when he arrived. "You sure about this?"

Clint looked her in the eye, "I am, are you?"

She didn't answer him, but instead started the boat's engine. They worked together to unfasten the ropes that secured the boat to the docks. When the boat slipped out to the open water, Clint took his bag of items he had purchased that morning down to the lower cabin.

The boat looked pretty much the same except a high-powered hunting rifle now rested against a corner of the cabin. He looked for anything else different but didn't see anything. He removed his Beretta and holster from his backpack and put them on.

Once he returned to the main deck, Mary called to him. "Come up here for a second."

Her voice sounded a little strange, and he noticed they seemed to be going further out from shore than she took them last time. He looked around but didn't see anything.

"Pour yourself some coffee, if you want some. I brought a thermos up here and a couple of cups. They're relatively clean."

"I saw you brought a rifle along this time. I don't want to have you do anything that will put you in harm's way."

"You're messing with a pit of vipers. I'll be keeping that rifle close for at least a week or two, and this thing," she motioned to the large revolver now holstered to her hip, "will stay attached for just as long."

"I want you to know something, Mary. I won't be coming back to the boat alone. She is in there. One of my photos I took last night caught her sitting outside before someone ordered her back in."

Mary's face paled. "Then I want to tell you something," she said with her voice softer than normal. She paused for a few seconds, like she was trying to catch her breath. "Fifteen years ago, not that long after I started my own charter business, and when this boat was still new to me, I took it into the waters near the fishery. It was in the middle of the day, a bright sunny day. I had already heard stories about the fishery and the men there, but I thought they were just scary tales."

She paused and studied the instrument panel. Clint didn't say anything.

"Two men in a small boat came along side. They both looked pleasant, smiled, and asked me if they could come on board and check out the boat. They said they hadn't seen it around before and thought it looked sharp. That was the term they used, sharp. I remember at the time, I knew I shouldn't have let them, but I did. Once on board they beat and raped me, afterwards I heard them laughing and talking about taking my boat out to sea where they could drop me in a spot where the current would take me further away from shore. No one would ever find me."

Mary paused, taking a sip of her coffee. She looked at Clint and almost smiled.

"I knew at the time the only reason they hadn't killed me was that they weren't done with me. That was their mistake. Even then I had this," she patted her revolver, "with me. I kept it in a drawer down below. Now, I keep it closer. I walked out of the cabin and shot them both. Just one shot each. I grew up shooting guns. We all do up here. There was very little emotion in it. I do remember that."

"One of them didn't die right away. He lay right there," she pointed to a spot on the steps near them. "He cried out in pain and kept apologizing, pleading with me to take him to a hospital. I remember thinking I needed to shoot him again, but I was worried the bullet might go through him and through the boat, making a hole in it. I didn't want a hole in my new boat."

"What did you do?"

"I let the boat continue on its way. I know the currents, too. When we reached the point where they would have tossed me overboard, I dropped them both into the water. Had to use the winch, but it wasn't hard. I think they were both dead by that time, but to be honest I didn't know and didn't care."

"No one can blame you, and certainly not me."

"It took me a long while to get over it. For several weeks, I cleaned and overhauled my boat but refused to take on any charters. Finally, I ran out of money. It was either go under or grow up. I chose to grow up. Became a bit paranoid on who I took out and always had one of the fish hands help out, so I wasn't alone. I slowly got back on my feet."

"Why did you take me out then, especially when you knew where I wanted to go?"

"I'm older, wiser, and can take better care of myself. It seemed obvious to me you were looking for someone or something, which you confirmed early on. When I learned it was the fishery, that did scare me. Still does, but I can't imagine how awful it would be for a woman to be a prisoner there."

"I try to block that out of my mind. Emotions don't help."

Mary nodded. She understood.

"The rifle?"

"If you defy the odds and make it back with them chasing you, or if you don't, and they come looking for your accomplices, I don't plan on letting them get anywhere near my boat."

"Don't come back to the drop-off spot until I contact you, and don't worry, they can't use or trace anything through my phone. I paid extra for a few security things," Clint said.

"I hope you make it back, but if you don't, at least hurt those bastards. Don't ever think because you surrender that they will let you go or the girl go. You both are as good as dead once you turn over your weapon. I've seen enough movies to know that."

Clint nodded, "Me, too."

In the darkness, Mary turned the boat parallel to shore and they headed toward the destination.

"I didn't want anyone back at the docks to know which way we were headed. They can't see us in the dark this far out. Only a few people live on this other side. Now we just have to trust modern technology to help get us to where we were yesterday."

Clint looked at the control panel. It reminded him of the cockpit of an airplane. "Ever wonder how the sailors of old got around?"

"All the time," she said, "and I still don't know if they were really brave or just really foolish. It's one thing to navigate, but not knowing the weather is suicidal. Even with all this I nearly got caught out in a major storm that came up fast. I could see

Skagway. I was real close and yet for a few moments, I didn't think we were going to make it."

"Hopefully, the weather will stay good tonight."

"It should," Mary said, "but the next few days the weather will be going downhill. So, get your business done tonight."

"You'll like her."

"Your friend?"

"Yes."

"I hope I get to meet her."

"Me, too."

A handful of clouds that seemed to be stuck in the air above the mountains blocked the light from the moon, making it hard to find the exact spot they landed on shore the day before, even with the assistance of GPS.

"Damn," Mary murmured as the small craft bounced off a large rock that barely touched the surface.

"Just over here," Clint said and pointed a little to their right. They both had agreed not to use any lights. A bit paranoid, Clint had thought. They were still about a mile away from the fishery and around the bend of shoreline, but he had sensed her dread of being there and didn't try to convince her a little light wouldn't hurt.

They separated with nothing more than a head nod by Clint. He disappeared into the forest, and Mary returned to her boat. She started the engine and moved the boat back in the direction of Skagway.

CHAPTER 37

Clint moved quicker than he did the night before, as he recognized and anticipated much of the terrain. When he neared the point where the chain link fence surrounded the fishery, an unexpected sound caused him to stop in his tracks. He caught movement about thirty yards ahead of him and down by the water.

He crouched and froze. A large bear and a cub appeared to be eating something on the water's edge. The adult bear stood up and looked around, and Clint wondered if the bear sensed he was there. Clint remained still, but considered backing away and detouring deeper into the woods before approaching the fishery. After a few seconds the big bear nudged the cub, and both jogged back into the forest.

He still didn't move, debating with himself how long he should wait to allow the bear to put some distance between itself and the fishery. As he waited, he saw another smaller creature leave the shelter of the forest and approach whatever the bears had been eating. A fox, he thought, and believed it to be a good omen. The fox wouldn't have approached the spot if it hadn't felt safe. Of course, Clint knew the fox could run a lot faster than he could if it had made a mistake. Still, Clint decided it was safe to move on.

He moved quietly around the compound to the gate nearest to where he had seen Frankie the night before. A space of about thirty feet had originally been cleared outside the entire fence line, but over time, a variety of small shrubs had grown up in the space. Whoever was responsible for keeping the area clear had done a half-assed job, Clint thought, as in some sections the cleared area had become much smaller. Nothing tall had been allowed to grow, but areas where the ground was rocky or had eroded over the years had definitely received less attention. This spot near the gate had been ignored too long. Even in daylight, a person could crawl within a few yards of the gate without being obvious to the casual observer.

Clint, of course, also had the advantage of darkness. He had no reason to believe the fishery had much of a security system. He thought he had seen security cameras out front facing the docks, but he had seen nothing in the back. He had not seen any signs of guards or dogs either.

His plan had him waiting until after midnight, by which time, he hoped everyone in the fishery would be asleep. The wait would give him an opportunity to watch for any activity and go over his plan a few more times in his mind. He had learned through his experience in the military and now in his current role that rushing into things rarely was a good idea, and he was already rushing things enough.

While Section had provided him with the blueprints of the fishery, they had not been able to develop any information about the personnel or activities there. In his last text Buzz said, "They only have an old landline listed as a means of contact, and it's only been used a couple of times in the last year. Finding out who is actually employed there is even harder. Everything is designed to delay pinpointing who does what, and perhaps more importantly, who gets paid what. We've got a few names, but none of them have anything listed anywhere else. It's like they are all off the grid."

Clint responded by texting, "Well this is Alaska." He didn't care about names. He would get in and out as quietly as possible. But he wouldn't come out without Frankie, and if that meant going through every living soul in there to get to her, he would do it.

The breeze picked up a little and sent a chill through him. Good, he thought, at least he wouldn't fall asleep while waiting in the dark. He wondered if the bear had left the area or was out there now, watching him the way he was watching the fishery, both waiting to attack. For some strange reason, the thought made him smile.

Somewhere in the back of his mind rose the question, "Why are you out here?" He squashed the thought and any lingering doubt. He owed her. His desire to uncover his treasure, there on the mesa outside Las Vegas, caused all this. He hadn't gone looking for it because some friend was pressing him to tell him what it was. No, he made the trip and dug up his treasure all on his own. Now, he had to try to fix the last thing that might still be fixable. He owed her, and he would rescue her or die trying.

Clouds began rolling in, and Clint wondered if Mary's weather forecast would hold. Moonshine came and went with the clouds' constant movement across the sky. He backed away a few yards during a period of total darkness and started taking things out of his backpack. First, he removed the night vision goggles and studied the gate and the nearest buildings. Satisfied that nothing had changed, he set the goggles down and removed his K-bar knife and fastened it under his jacket to his belt. Next, he took out what the Hollywood crowd would call a silencer, modified specifically for his Beretta. There isn't anything that will totally silence a gunshot, the noise is only suppressed, but they do help.

After attaching the "silencer", he dug deeper into his backpack and found a small, but very powerful flashlight and placed it in his jacket pocket. He inventoried the few remaining items and satisfied, he set the backpack on the ground. He would not take it in with him.

Twenty minutes later, as Clint took one last glance with the night vision goggles to ensure nothing had changed, a small branch broke somewhere behind him in the forest. He turned and looked into the forest. With the goggles on he could see movement in the distance but too many trees and the thick underbrush prevented him from getting a clear view. Something big, perhaps the bear, or an elk, or a moose, he thought. The large animal must have stepped on something that had fallen to the ground.

He didn't feel threatened, but the sight of a large animal moving around behind him reminded him he wasn't alone in the forest and reinforced his desire to get the job done and out of these woods. He laid the goggles on top of the backpack.

The clouds floated under the moon, blocking the little light the moon provided. Clint crawled to the gate in the darkness and after verifying one last time that no one was out and about, he went up and over the six-foot gate. Once inside, he spent twenty seconds picking the simple dead bolt that secured the gate shut. He didn't know if anyone could tell if the lock was missing from the gate by looking out the window or coming outside for a smoke break, so he left the lock in place. He felt certain in the darkness no one could tell that the lock was open.

Dashing to the same door in which the man took Frankie, Clint stopped, crouched, and looked around one last time outside. He reached for the door handle, hoping it would not be locked. It turned and the door opened.

CHAPTER 38

The inside of the building was as dark as the outside, making Clint wonder if he had made a mistake by leaving the night vision goggles outside. The goggles would give him an advantage, but they also would render him blind for seconds if someone turned on a light. In those few seconds, that someone could easily kill him. He would use the darkness as an ally, letting his eyes get accustomed to it, and use his flashlight sparingly.

He also figured that if someone heard him or became suspicious, they would turn on a light and that would give him a heads up. Gripping his pistol in his right hand and the small flashlight still turned off in his other hand, he crept down the hallway. He found the first door on his left open, and glancing in, he thought the door led into a storage room. He stepped into the room and turned on the flashlight to verify the room was empty.

Turning the flashlight off, he left the room, and as he did, he noticed the room and even the hallway become a little less dark. Glancing back, he noticed the window had brightened as light from the moon now shown through it. He wondered how long the break in the clouds would last. The scant light made getting around a lot easier.

Two more empty rooms had their doors open to the hallway. He paused for a second at each to look inside. At the end of the hall, he found a closed door to his right. Immediately in front of him, he saw a large room with two long tables in the middle of the room and a long counter against the wall. Boxes or crates were stacked on the far side of the room. He used the flashlight long enough to verify no one was in the large room, which he now thought was where they might process the fish they caught.

He turned his attention to the closed door and opened it. The door opened without making a noise, and Clint immediately saw a man asleep on a bed inside.

"Bingo," he said to himself. The man resembled the person that led Frankie indoors the night before. Clint took four quick steps and brought the butt of the pistol down on the man's nose.

"Ahh!" the man gasped and flailed around wildly to sit up. He put a hand up to his nose, and Clint jabbed the man's hand and nose with his left fist, still wrapped around the flashlight. "Help!" the man called out in a voice that sounded more like he was talking in his sleep than really shouting for help.

"Quiet or you die," Clint said loud enough to get the man's attention. The man's eyes finally focused on Clint, and he saw the pistol.

"Who are you?" he asked.

"I'm here for the woman. That's all I want. Take me to her now, and I'll spare your life."

The man smiled, and for a moment, Clint thought he might start laughing. "You're insane. You came here for her. She ain't the same, Jack. You'd be smart to start running away now and hope they don't find you."

While a small part of Clint wondered who "they" were, he knew he had to keep his focus and move quickly. "Take me to her now."

"Okay, okay. You have to let me up and don't get mad at

me when you see her," the man grinned. "Hell, I haven't even had my turn with her yet."

Clint backed away a step from the bed, and the man rolled over as he began to get up. Clint saw his hand reach for something and was about to say something when the man struck like a snake with a knife. Clint tucked his stomach back as the blade caught his jacket and shot the man in the chest. The man looked at Clint for a second, confusion in his eyes, before falling to the floor.

Clint didn't check the body to see if he was dead. He saw where the bullet entered the chest and knew the man no longer posed a threat. He left the room, hoping that the little noise that he had made in the room had gone unnoticed. A quick glance into the hallway didn't reveal the presence of anyone else. The large room only had two windows, but he could see enough to work his way to a hallway straight across from him. As he crossed the large room, he noticed the entrance to another hallway leading from the room to his right. He continued to the hall straight ahead of him.

It turned out to be a short hall with just two doors. The first, to his left had been left partially open. He pushed the door to open it the rest of the way.

"AAYYYE!" A small form screamed and leapt at Clint. He saw something shiny reflect a moonbeam as it came down at his head. In the split second that the attack took, his attacker seemed to be flying behind the weapon.

The doorway limited Clint's options. Startled, he followed his instincts and took a step backwards, maintaining separation as the weapon barely missed striking him. Clint fired one round at point blank range into the flying figure. Despite this the figure landed on his legs, and the weapon, which Clint now recognized as a meat cleaver, struck at him a second time. Clint moved his foot as the blade grazed his shoe and struck the concrete floor. His attacker still lay face down, showing no signs of life, but the hand lifted the blade again. Clint took another step backwards and recognized his attacker as a woman. He fired again.

"By far, the deadlier of the species," he mumbled to himself and hurried to the next door. He knew someone else had to be coming.

This door had a sliding lock on the outside. He slid the lock out of its clasp and opened the door. He saw her. She didn't look the same, but he knew it was her even in the dark. He ran to her.

"Frankie, it's me, Clint," he whispered.

She sat in the corner of the room on the floor with her arms wrapped around her bent legs. She didn't move right away, but when he reached her, she jumped to her feet.

"Clint," she stammered.

"Yes, we've got to go." He didn't need to say more. She grabbed his arm and pulled him, leading them both out of the room, down the hall, and straight across the large room the way Clint had arrived.

"Hey! Stop!" A man shouted from their left near the third doorway to the big room. He began running at them and had something like a baseball bat in his hand.

Clint shot him twice before he made it halfway to them. Frankie tugged at his arm again and the two began running. Clint led her outside through the door and to the gate, where they had to pause to pull off the unlatched lock and swing the gate open. As they did, the sudden blast from a high-powered rifle and simultaneous loud ring from the metal gate post next to them brought them both to their knees.

Clint spun and fired several rounds at the dark figure. He didn't stop firing until the man collapsed to the ground and the Beretta ran out of bullets. The person had stood too far away for Clint to be sure of his aim with the pistol, but he knew the odds were good that at least one round had struck the man.

"Please," Frankie urged and tugged at Clint's arm again.

The moon broke through the clouds, casting a dim light around them, and Clint knew they had to get to the cover of the nearby trees. They scrambled to the spot where Clint had left the backpack. He had to pull on Frankie to stop her from running.

"A minute only," he said. "You can't run through this terrain barefoot."

"You'd be surprised what I could do to get away from here," she said almost in a snarl.

"Please," he whispered and dumped the contents of the backpack onto the ground. He separated the shoes. "Here, put these on and anything else you need."

Clint reloaded his pistol before grabbing the night vision goggles to study the compound and the area inside and outside the fence. He didn't see anyone, and that made him uncomfortable. He would rather see everyone running out into the open where he could pick them off one by one, or at least do some more damage. He had the ominous feeling that someone inside had taken charge and had come up with a better plan to come after him.

"Let's go," Frankie pleaded.

Clint looked at her and saw that she had removed what she had on and put on the black sweat suit and the walking shoes.

"Did you bring me a gun?"

"No, but I guess I should've."

"Give me something. I'm not going back in there."

In the moonlight and as close as they were to each other, he could see what had only been impressions before. A large knot almost had her right eye closed and the right half of her lower lip had swollen twice its size. Her hair had been cut short.

"I won't let that happen. Stay close, and if I go down you can have my Beretta."

She gave him a slight nod, and the two started walking as fast as Clint thought safe in the darkness. They stayed a little deeper in the woods than he had before when he had made the trips back and forth, but they still kept the compound in sight. When they reached the spot where the shore ran away from the fishery and where he had seen the bear and her cub, a buzzing in the air caught Clint's attention.

In less than a second, he knew what made the sound. He grabbed Frankie, pulled her to the ground under a large tree and tried to hold her close. For more than a second, she struggled to get away.

"It's a drone. Stay still."

She suddenly stopped fighting him and started crying softly.

"They'll be looking for two people moving. We'll look like one large animal curled up under a tree," he said. He looked at her, but she had curled up in a fetal position and had her eyes closed. He had a sudden urge to go back to the compound and kill everyone. What hell had she gone through, he thought, but blocked the images that came to mind. They would do him or her no good.

"Rage does you no good," a grizzled old sergeant had once told him. "Sure, it gives you strength and purpose, but it steals away your reasoning. You miss critical items that will only lead to an early death, and your adversary will win again. There's an old saying I like, 'Revenge is a dish best served cold'."

Clint had made it a point to never forget that advice. The drone didn't seem to slow down as it passed overhead, and he hoped that meant the camera missed them. Better that than coming back for a closer look.

He saw a spotlight searching the water in front of the fishery and then being turned to inspect the shoreline in their direction. The light only searched as far as the edge of the water. When it went back to searching the water in front of the fishery, he tugged at Frankie.

"Let's move."

She didn't need a second prompt. The two started hiking away from the compound, making good time for about a minute before the moon ducked behind the clouds and their surroundings darkened even more.

"Be careful, it's easy to trip out here."

"Just keep moving," Frankie said, and Clint sensed anger in her voice. He decided to walk a little faster, realizing that she'd rather trip a dozen times than have anyone from the fishery catch up with them.

"How many people were at the fishery?" Clint asked.

"I don't know. I was kept in the room, unless the bastard wanted me."

Clint didn't want to follow up on that comment. Stay cool,

he told himself. They walked for another five minutes with the sound of the small waves striking the rocky beach breaking the relative silence. The screech of an owl in a tree above them brought both to a crouch. He glanced back at Frankie, and she nodded, motioning with her hand for them to keep going.

They continued on course, but after a few minutes, Clint heard the engine of a small boat racing toward them. For the second time the two curled together behind a large tree trunk. Clint peered around the tree as the boat with two men on board went by, a good fifty yards offshore. He had an uneasy feeling that the drone had spotted Mary and her boat.

CHAPTER 39

Clint and Frankie resumed their trek, staying closer to the shoreline, so as to not get lost. The clouds had gotten thicker and lower, making any further help from the moon unlikely.

"Careful, the terrain is really bad here and will be for the next fifty or so yards. Easy to break an ankle."

Frankie didn't answer him. He looked back at her, but she didn't make eye contact. She kept her left hand stretched in front of her gently on his right elbow. His mind could sense her thoughts, "Just keep moving, keep moving."

At times, the trees grew right up to the edge of the water. If they didn't, they usually left an open space of no more than ten yards to the edge of the water. In a few spots, however, because the way the shore was shaped, or because of the number of large boulders that seemed to be trying to make their slow escape from the water, the treeless gap could be as much as twenty-five yards. The large boulders provided some cover, too, if a person happened to be on the right side of one when confronted.

If the clouds hadn't been so thick, the moon may have provided enough light for Clint to have recognized the spot a few yards before they reached it and detoured around it by staying in the trees. However, in the darkness, he stepped out into the open and immediately paused, sensing as much as observing movement to his left by the water. He looked and saw a man standing next to a boat that had been pulled up to the edge of the shoreline. The man watched Clint appear out of the trees and raised what appeared to be a rifle, aiming it at them. Clint brought his Beretta up and fired two shots as the rifle also roared in the night.

Clint felt a sting and a slight tug on his pants. He instinctively dropped to one knee forming a smaller target, and he would have fired the 9mm again except for seeing the man crumble to the ground. He moved quickly to the man to ensure he still didn't pose a threat. He didn't. Bending over to pick up the man's rifle, he heard Frankie gasp and the crunching of small rocks and pebbles behind him. He spun, only to be hit by a large, powerful form that Clint first thought was the bear.

The impact almost knocked him senseless as he, and what he now realized was a man, ricocheted off the boat's bow and rolled to the edge of the water. The huge man grabbed at Clint's right wrist and twisted, causing Clint's Beretta to fly off into the dark water and almost snapping Clint's wrist. The man tried to get a grip on Clint with his other hand, but he was out of position, and Clint hit the man's elbow as hard as he could with his left hand. Clint hoped the blow would do damage to the man's elbow, but other than allowing Clint to break the grip on his wrist, the man seemed unphased.

His assailant jabbed at Clint striking him on the cheek, and despite being off balance and now on his knees, the big guy's punch rocked Clint, who was doing his best to separate himself further from the man. They both got to their feet, and Clint got his first good look at Chappie. The man had to be a good six foot six and weighed close to three hundred pounds. Worse yet, even in the darkness, Clint could tell Chappie had the build of a linebacker on a pro football team and not like someone who may have gotten his size from eating a few too many cheeseburgers at the bowling alley.

"You're a fool, kid," Chappie said. "I hope they're paying you big, and that you aren't here because you're lovesick. Not that it matters, cause you're going to die here tonight."

Clint took advantage of Chappie's little speech by getting his head to stop spinning and the feeling back into his right hand.

"It's over, you know. Your whole operation, the Chinese connection, it's done. I'm just here to get the girl out before the feds crash in on you." Clint wanted to get Chappie thinking of something else and stall the fight a few seconds longer. If his words affected Chappie, Clint couldn't tell. The man looked to be in his forties, and even in the darkness, Clint could see the confidence in his face. A confidence that had come from experience, no doubt, and that would make him more dangerous.

"Maybe I won't kill you tonight. Maybe I'll just break a few bones and take you back with me to get everything you know out of you, and for you to watch me and the bitch get it on some more." Chappie said as he slowly circled Clint, and Clint realized the man wanted to get him with his back to the water.

Clint moved sideways to avoid the trap, and Chappie charged. Clint's years of training kicked in, and he dodged the charge, kicking hard at the man's knee as he went by. Chappie didn't move as fast or was as well trained in martial arts, but he knew how to fight, and he was strong, very strong. He swatted at Clint's leg just as it made contact with his knee, deflecting most of the impact.

Chappie stood up and shook his leg. "That was nothing,

boy. I can do this all night, and you know the girl has already run off into the woods. I guess she doesn't want to see you die."

Clint knew Frankie had left, and he hoped she would keep running until she ran into someone who could take her to safety. Clint looked down at the rifle on the ground. Chappie watched his eyes and took a couple steps to the rifle. Clint thought he would pick the rifle up, and he couldn't let that happen, but to his surprise Chappie kicked the rifle into the water.

Chappie charged, and Clint again sidestepped and backed up avoiding the man's grasp. Chappie moved like a wrestler, Clint thought, with a goal of getting a grip on his opponent that would allow him to use his overpowering strength.

Clint glanced around, wondering if his best move might be to run. Chappie read his mind, most likely very use to his opponents trying to run away.

"You won't get far. I know these woods like the back of my hand. You'll go around in circles while my men and I track you down." He lunged again at Clint, getting a massive paw on Clint's shoulder. Clint ducked under him and drove his left fist into Chappie's side. Normally, he would have followed up with another punch, but his fist felt like it had just hit an oak tree, and Chappie was turning and reaching for him.

Clint jumped back and almost fell in the process. Chappie dove at him, and both once again rolled around on the ground. This time, Chappie was able to get an arm around Clint's head. He squeezed and the immense pressure was instant. Clint tried to shake him off, but Chappie laughed out loud, standing and picking Clint up off the ground by his head.

"Hell, your girl had more fight in her," he laughed again.

Clint hadn't forgotten about his knife. He simply didn't

want to expose it and have Chappie swat it away like a toy. Knowing the man wanted to get him in close for the kill, he had saved the knife as a last resort. He drew the knife and in one swift motion drove it into the Chappie's side under the ribs.

Chappie roared but didn't release Clint. With his vision beginning to blur, Clint continued to press in with the knife while slicing across Chappie's belly. He big man snarled and tossed Clint away from him. Clint hit the rocks on the ground hard, but forced himself back to his feet, staggering a few steps backward until his feet hit the cold water. He watched as Chappie stood there stunned, studying the gaping wound in his belly.

"It's over, Chappie. Give up, lie down, and I'll call 911."

Chappie charged him again. Clint brought the knife up expecting Chappie to stop, but the giant kept coming and grabbed Clint's knife hand just as the knife started to pierce Chappie's chest. He jerked Clint's arm up and then down spinning Clint around lake a ragdoll. Two thirds the way around a full spin he let go, and Clint bounced and rolled over the small rocks until he slammed against a large boulder.

He tried to push off the wet ground and instantly realized his right wrist might be broken. Worse yet, Chappie stood there grinning down at him. The man should be dead by now, Clint thought. He looked around for his knife but didn't see it in the dark and realized now may be the time to start running. Time was his ally. He just needed to stay away from Chappie's grasp until the man bled out. He got to his knees, but dizziness made him stop.

"Maybe it's time for you and me to take a swim," Chappie said in a voice that didn't sound like him.

Clint reached into his pocket and pulled out the small flashlight, shining it into Chappie's face. The man raised a hand to block the light and took an unsteady step forward. Clint brought the light down to the large belly wound and saw that blood covered most of Chappie's body below the wound and blood was still streaming out of the gash.

Suddenly a rock the size of a baseball sailed through the air and struck Chappie on the shoulder. The big man turned his head, grinned, and collapsed to the ground face down. Clint looked in the direction where the rock had come and saw Frankie standing about ten yards away. She had another larger rock in her hand, but rather than throw it, she rushed Chappie and started beating his head with the rock.

Clint forced himself to stand up. He ached all over, and since the cold water had gotten through his clothes, he began to shiver. He watched as Frankie repeatedly smashed the softball size rock into Chappie's head. Everything was eerily quiet, except for Frankie's grunts every time she brought the rock down on the dead man's head.

"Frankie, he's dead. Let's go. We have a boat to catch."

She looked up at Clint before bringing the rock down one more time on what was left of Chappie's skull. Frankie dropped the rock and looked at her hands.

"Wash them off in the water," Clint said, his voice soft.

Frankie stood up and swayed before getting her balance. She staggered the few yards to the water where she knelt and washed her hands. Clint thought he could hear her crying. He searched the ground and found his knife. His Beretta was lost in the dark water. He used his flashlight in a futile attempt to locate it.

"Are you ready? We do need to start moving." Clint thought about the small boat, but it had drifted about ten yards out into the water and was moving slowly away from them.

"Yes. I'm fine," Frankie said, but he knew she wasn't. She splashed water on her face and then stood up. "Are you hurt?"

"Nothing serious." He reached for her hand with his left hand, and she let him take it. He moved his right hand around and decided the wrist, despite being painful, would be alright.

"Should we try to get the boat?" she asked.

"Best to continue on foot, besides I'm already wet in a few spots. I don't want to get totally wet out here tonight."

"How about them," Frankie asked.

"Yeah, we better move them out of sight." Clint moved the smaller man into the trees, but when he got to Chappie, he found it almost impossible to move him. To his surprise Frankie joined him, and both grabbed a hand to drag him behind the nearest boulder. As they stepped away from Chappie's body, Frankie spit on him.

They continued their hike around the corner of the inlet. When they came within a few hundred yards of the spot where Clint expected to meet Mary, he thought he heard something or someone following them. His first thought was the bear, but he believed it was more likely to be someone else from the fishery. He began to wish they had looked for the rifle Chappie had kicked into the water.

CHAPTER 40

"Thank you," Frankie said. They had walked in silence for over ten minutes, and her remark caught Clint off guard. "For what?"

"Don't be stupid, for rescuing me. I had given up all hope. One part of my mind still thinks I'm back there and this is a dream, but then I think of Chappie's ugly, fat head and how good it felt to hit it with that rock. Thank you for that, too."

Therapy comes in many forms, Clint thought. "I had to find you."

"Did, um, what's his name, Buzz help?

"Yes, they all did."

"But you came by yourself?"

"Yes. That's how it works."

"Well, tell him thanks, too."

"I will."

A twig snapped behind them. They both stopped. Clint put his finger to his lips, and Frankie nodded. "Let's walk a little faster," he whispered.

They moved a little quicker, but running was impossible in the darkness and the rough terrain. When they approached the rendezvous point, Clint stopped and kneeled behind a tree. Frankie joined him. After listening for ten seconds and not hearing anything, he took his phone out of his pocket and sent a prearranged text to Mary.

"Who is that to?" Frankie asked in a voice so soft Clint barely heard her.

"Our ride out of here."

Clint periodically checked the map on his phone to guide them to the exact spot for the rendezvous with Mary. He sensed someone was out there watching and following him, but he didn't see or hear anything more to confirm his suspicions.

Once at the meeting point, he saw the small raft, but no sign of Mary. They walked down to the shore and looked around.

"Should we call for someone?" Frankie asked.

"Not yet," Clint said. He looked around again. Nearby large boulders could conceal someone, but unless she had fallen asleep, which he didn't think likely, she should have noticed their approach. The last twenty yards they would have been in plain view and walking on the rocks made enough noise to awaken a light sleeper. What if they had gotten here already and had Mary somewhere?

A sudden loud blast of gunfire startled Clint and Frankie. Pieces of rock scattered around their feet.

"Don't move or your dead."

The man was a good fifteen yards away, coming out of the tree line and waving a handgun of some sort at them. If Clint had his Beretta, he might have taken the chance that he could outshoot the man, but all he had was the knife. No good at all at this distance, and the man was walking toward them to get into better range.

The man fired again and rocks shattered so close to his feet that Clint involuntarily lifted his right foot up as small fragments slammed and cut into his ankle. Clint took one small step toward the nearest large boulders. A few rose to eight or nine feet and would offer good, albeit temporary protection.

The man raised his firearm and moved closer to the

boulders, cutting off Clint's only chance of cover. "Don't move! I want to talk, and I have no reason to kill the woman. Any attempt to escape and you both die. Understand?"

"Yes. You're the man I saw with the coin, aren't you?" Clint asked finally recognizing him in the darkness. "Why are you threatening us?"

"Silly question. I want to know who you are and why you are here?"

"I came looking for Frankie," Clint said and nodded toward her. "That's all. Nothing to do with you. What are you even doing out here?"

"Forgive me, but I don't believe you. You couldn't have traced her here on your own, and a man fitting your description was with her in Las Vegas. I know who she is."

"Then you should know I'm just her boyfriend."

"Too skillful of a boyfriend for me."

"Look, I spent time in the military. I know my way around weapons, but I'm no threat to anyone here in Alaska." Clint knew the man had come from the fishery, but he didn't want to confirm that to him.

"Ha. You killed most of the people back there already. Was that you that did Chappie?"

"You mean that big thug who attacked us?" Clint said.

"I have to give you credit. I've known him for years, and no one has ever beaten him in a fight, even with a knife, not even close."

"He got stupid, and I got lucky."

"Who smashed his head in? Was that you, Frankie? Couldn't blame you. I admit I often felt like going in there and shooting him for what he was doing to you. All the screams and crying, I had to go outside and get away from it all. The man was sick."

"Then why didn't you?" Frankie asked. The bitterness in her voice couldn't be concealed.

"Bigger picture, my dear, bigger picture. We needed him, and if it wasn't you, it would just be someone else. I can't begin to tell you how many women, hell girls, are buried out back. The man was sick, real sick, but he was a very big help to us. Besides you were as good as dead once we killed the FBI agent."

"You're not making sense. What are you doing avoiding taxes, illegal fishing? This is crazy," Clint said.

"I don't know if you are as stupid as you are acting, or if you think you're fooling me. You know, I might actually believe you, if you hadn't shown that interest in my coin."

Clint didn't say anything, but knew the man had put a lot together already.

"Why was the coin of interest?"

"Shiny and pretty," Clint said. "I'm a collector."

"Okay, let's get serious. You tell me who you are and what you know about me and the business we're doing here. You get, what?" he paused and Clint could tell he was enjoying himself. "Ten seconds, and then I shoot your lady friend in the leg. Then we go to five, and I shoot you in the leg. We can keep this going for a while, I have plenty of bullets."

"Hold on," Clint said.

"Ten, nine, eight-"

"You know I'm a police officer," Frankie shouted.

"Who cares. Seven, six---"

"He is, too. We're both with the Las Vegas Police Department."

"Nope. I know he had just come into town. Both the lawyer and his assistant verified that, although she took a little more encouraging."

"You?" Frankie asked. "You killed my partner, too."

"The cop outside the door? No, that wasn't me. Willy did him, I just did the other two. At the time I needed to know a few things. Now they don't matter."

"But why? Why do all this?" Frankie asked.

He smiled. He was still too far for Clint to rush but too close to miss them when he started shooting. Clint considered jumping into the water, but he knew for the first ten feet or so the water was too shallow to provide any real cover.

"Who do you think brought you here, Frankie? I still can't believe how much trouble it was. More important to me though, is how do you think they traced you here?"

Frankie stared at the man, and Clint thought she was considering charging at him. Maybe if they both did, one of them might actually reach him.

"You brought me here? How can you be so cruel?"

"I thought I'd already explained that. Now you can tell me how they knew you were here? Or you can, Clint. That is your name, right? If my memory is right, that's the name you gave the lawyer."

"My name is Clint, and what's yours?"

"Damn, we should break out the tea and have a party now that we are all friends." He grinned and moved the gun back into position to shoot at one of Frankie's legs.

"It would be better than this," Clint said.

"Please don't kill us," Frankie pleaded.

That brought a grin to the man's face. "Maybe in our next

life we can all be friends. Now, where was I? Eight, seven, six, five, four, he took aim, three—"

The blast of the revolver shattered the silence, and both Frankie and Clint dove and started scrambling for cover. A second and third roar from Mary's .45 exploded in the night and were followed by echoes of the gunshots and the sound of birds and other wildlife fleeing the area around them.

Mary walked out of the shadows and stood over the dead body. Clint thought she might shoot him one more time, and she did.

CHAPTER 41

Mary looked at Clint and the girl. "You made it. I never believed you had a chance."

"Almost didn't, thank you," Clint said, walking up to her. Frankie didn't move.

"I didn't know if I could shoot him," Mary said. "I saw him behind you as you got close. I was up there watching for you." She motioned with her free hand at a small slope topped with two large rocks that rose up out of the ground. "I didn't know how to warn you, either."

"Well, you did the right thing. I don't know if there's anyone else coming, but we better go, don't you think?"

"Yes, but shouldn't we do something with him?" Mary asked. "I'd rather not try to explain this to the police."

"I'll drag him back into the trees. I know there's a few hungry animals in there. You know, circle of life and all that." He didn't wait for an answer, dragging the dead man off. Before he left him, he took a photo of the man, removed and photographed the man's ID documents from his wallet, and dug the gold coin out of the man's pocket."

He sent the picture via text to Buzz. When he came back out of the woods, Mary and Frankie were huddled together talking.

"Ready?" Clint asked.

"Been ready," Mary said. The three climbed into the small raft, and Mary steered it out into the darkness toward the awaiting boat. A light mist had begun falling, and the clouds began to merge with the sea.

Clint worried about their ability to find the boat with the fog and the darkness, but Mary must have linked in the GPS coordinates to her phone, watch, or something as in less than three minutes, they were bumping up against the boat.

"For now, let's leave this tied up to the boat while we get moving out of here," Mary said, as Clint was getting into position to help Mary bring it onboard. "It's foggy now, but I still want to make sure there's nothing out here looking for us."

"Fine by me," Frankie said in a voice so soft Clint almost didn't hear her. She walked to the side of the boat and grabbed the handrail with both hands, staring out into the fog.

"Come give me a hand," Mary said to Clint. She led him into the small pilot's cabin and started the boat's engine. "You know just because she's free of them, she's really not." Clint didn't immediately respond, and Mary continued. "She's going to need therapy. Someone to talk to, and trust me, it can't be you."

Clint first reaction was to become defensive, but he knew she was right. He could listen, but he didn't have the slightest clue as to what he should say.

"Don't misunderstand me. She'll want you close, but she'll need someone else to talk to. In my case, I would want a woman. Her opinion of men right now may not be very great. That means no matter how close you two were in the past, don't expect or push for that relationship to start back up anytime soon."

"I can certainly appreciate that," Clint said. "I didn't come up here to save her for me. I came here to save her for her."

She smiled at him. "You're a good man, Clint, now go and

stand next to her. Main thing is for her to know you're there. Besides, it doesn't look like there are any other ships out here now to worry about."

"Thanks, Mary. You know, there may be someone still alive back there. If there are, they might come looking for who did this to them. I can help you go on a vacation somewhere until this dies down."

"We'll see. What happened to the big guy? That's the one everyone I know is afraid of?"

"He's dead."

"Without him the rest of them will likely just disappear. The guy I shot seemed to be the other guy who had pull, at least with the group whenever they came into town. The big guy rarely came into town, but the guy I shot was in now and then. The others treated him as though he was their leader."

"Let's hope you're right and everyone else disappears on their own. I better check on Frankie," Clint said and walked over to her.

"You like boats?" Clint asked her.

"Can we leave tonight? Get as far away as possible?" Frankie asked, ignoring his question.

"Yes, that's the plan. The car's packed and ready to go. We'll go straight to the car and drive away."

"Good." She stared out into the fog for a moment, before leaving him at the rail and walking up to Mary.

Clint watched her. Frankie showed Mary her sleeve, and the two came to some sort of agreement. A few seconds later, the two went down the steps into the cabin below. Clint knew Mary had said earlier that the boat could steer itself for a while, but the boat plowing through the small waves in the dark fog with no one at the helm gave him an eerie feeling.

About a minute later, Mary returned from below. She again motioned for Clint to follow her, and he did.

"She's been beaten badly, Clint. I'm not talking about her face either. Have you seen her with that sweatshirt off?"

"No," Clint felt the anger growing in him again.

Mary shook her head. "I can't comprehend how someone can be so evil. And I heard that guy said there were bodies buried back there." She shook her head again. "May he roast in hell. May all of them roast in hell."

"I have a way to get the police out there that won't implicate either of us, Mary. We'll let them know about the bodies. It may be a day or two, but we'll put closure on this."

"Good. Their families need it." Mary shook her head slowly. "I'm giving her one of my flannel shirts. The sweatshirt is covered with blood."

"The blood is from Chappie, the big guy."

"Did she kill him?"

"No, I think he was already dead. Here, I want you to have this," Clint handed her the gold coin he took from the man. "It's genuine and worth more than its weight in gold."

"You already more than paid me."

"Maybe, but this is part of the treasure I discovered that caused all this. Now that it's over, I want you to have it. It will help bring closure to me."

Mary looked at the coin in her hand and dropped it into her pants pocket. "Go check on her. We still have fifteen minutes or so before we get there."

Clint found Frankie sitting on a chair staring into a small mirror. She had on a brown and green checkered flannel shirt that looked a size too small for her.

"I don't want to go back to Las Vegas."

"You don't have to," Clint said.

"I need to let them know I'm alive and free, but I don't want to talk about this. I don't want everyone to know what happened to me. I don't want to see a doctor, and I don't want to talk about this. I don't want anyone touching me. I want to forget."

Clint knew forgetting was not an option, but he could help with the rest. "Hey, look at me, please." She did. "I can make all that happen. No one will bother you, and no one, I mean that, no one will touch you."

"We'll drive out of this place tonight and never stop?"

"How about we stop in the middle of nowhere?"

"Okay," Frankie said, giving him a half-hearted smile.

CHAPTER 42

"This kind of wraps things up," Buzz said.

"Think so? Sometimes there are layers hidden under layers," Deer said.

"I know, but this guy," he handed a slim folder to Deer with the picture of the man Mary had shot on the rocky shore a few nights before paperclipped to the cover, "he brought us a whole new batch of information."

"Summarize."

"He owned an import export business with customers that include a variety of legitimate and not so legitimate U.S. businesses. One was the fishery up near Skagway. His main client appears to be the Chinese government. The anonymous tip we passed on to the FBI that he was behind the killing of their agent and the kidnapping of Frankie sent them into a feeding frenzy. They've got the IRS and the Trade Commission digging into the company, too."

"Couldn't happen to a nicer guy."

"You know, Clint says his discovery, or his treasure as he calls it, caused nothing but harm. He blames himself for the deaths and for what happened to Frankie."

"I can certainly understand that, even though none of it was his fault."

"Yeah, but what he doesn't appreciate is what a coup it was for the U.S. We never would've discovered the land purchases by the Chinese or the identity of so many Chinese agents and shell companies operating here. This has turned out big, real big."

"I don't disagree with you, but you can't expect Clint to see anything but Frankie right now, and for that he blames himself. Probably always will. You've been staying in touch?"

"Yes. Not much, just the occasional text."

"Make sure he knows he's still on an extended vacation that's on our dime, and then, Buzz, tell Dolly to keep in contact with him. I want you to focus on what is going on in Africa. Leave Clint to her. Okay?"

"Sure."

"And send Dolly in here for a minute."

Buzz left, and a few seconds later Dolly entered Deer's office.

"Dolly, I want you to take over communications with Clint. With what he's dealing with now, I think having a woman at this end talking to him would be a lot better for him."

"I understand, boss."

"You know he's out of his depth with this. I can't imagine going through what she has gone through, and we know he has no experience in helping out in situations like this. Get him to talk to you. He needs to vent now and then, too."

"Will do," Dolly said.

"Thanks," Deer said.

Dolly started to leave and turned. "New boyfriend, Boss?"

"What?"

"Well, new hair, dressier clothes, a more confident walk, and a hint of a smile when no one is looking?"

"Get that smirk off your face and get out of here," Deer said, but couldn't keep the grin off her own face.

CHAPTER 43

The small flat-bottom fishing boat moved slowly through Lake Babine. Frankie sat in front of Clint facing him and holding a fishing pole off to the side of the boat. The line pulled a spinner behind the boat as they trolled for the large fish below them. They had only caught a couple of fish since arriving three days earlier. Clint faced forward and steered the boat by turning the small motor from side to side.

She was quiet, as she pretty much had been since they left Skagway four days before. They had gotten across the border into Canada without a problem. Of course, it was long after midnight, and the lone border agent was likely at the end of his shift.

Their morning arrival at the lodge surprised Rex, the manager, but he welcomed both of them with open arms and gave them a private cabin. Clint thought he saw a look of concern in Rex's eyes when he looked at Frankie. He couldn't help but see the bruising and swelling that was still there.

Clint thought about saying something but didn't want to in front of Frankie. She didn't need two men talking about what happened to her. So, he wasn't really surprised when there was a knock on their cabin door a few minutes after they got to the cabin. Clint opened the door and found a woman in her sixties with greying hair and a big smile carrying two bath towels.

"Hi, I'm Jolene with housekeeping. I wanted to make sure everything was made up here and check one thing in the bathroom."

"Sure, come in, Jolene." Clint had little doubt that Rex had suggested she come check on Frankie. Maybe that was a good thing. "Frankie," Clint turned to Frankie who was still standing in the middle of the room looking nervous. "I've got to run to the car and get the rest of our stuff. This is Jolene with housekeeping. She'll just be in and out. Is that okay?"

The pause before she answered didn't surprise Clint, but he knew it would catch Jolene's attention.

"Want me to help?" Frankie asked.

"No, I'll be quick," Clint said and left.

He wondered if he should delay his return to the cabin, but decided that it was too early to test Frankie. He grabbed the last few items and was back in the cabin within two minutes. He didn't expect what he found. Both women were hugging and crying in the middle of the room. The towels were sitting on a nearby table.

"Should I come back?" Clint asked.

Frankie nodded, and after seeing that, Jolene said, "Yes. Tell Rex to buy you a beer at the bar."

The bar wasn't open, but he found Rex sitting at the counter reading a book. "Jolene said for you to buy me a beer."

Rex grinned. "You knew I sent her, didn't you?"

"Yes, but I don't blame you."

"Do we need to know anything? I mean like are you on the run? Is someone after her or you now?"

"I don't believe so, but if anyone comes around asking, let me know right away."

"Should I inform the police?" Rex asked.

"No, she would be furious if we did that. She doesn't want to talk to anyone about it, although she and Jolene seemed to have hit it off. Besides what happened to her happened in Alaska."

"Guess we have to respect her wishes, but I hate to think someone got away with beating a woman and ...," Rex didn't finish his sentence, but Clint knew what he was inferring.

"He didn't."

Rex looked at Clint as though he wanted to ask a follow up question; however, the conversation turned to fishing, and Rex mentioned that a bear had been sighted near the lodge. Clint said he wasn't sure how long they'd be staying, but he hoped it would be for at least three or four days.

Jolene showed up about ten minutes later. "I told her I would send you back," she said.

"Ok, I'd better get back there."

"And, Clint, thank you," she said.

He left the bar imagining Jolene would quickly fill Rex in with whatever information she had gotten from Frankie. He found Frankie sitting in a chair with her hands on her head staring at the floor when he returned to the room.

"Are you okay?"

"Yes. No, I'm a mess. I need to take a shower but didn't want to until you were back. I was never afraid before. I need a shower, but I was too scared to take one until you were back," she repeated. A few tears reappeared in her eyes.

"I'm back now. Go take a nice, long shower."

"She asked me if you did this to me."

"Jolene?" he asked, even though he knew it couldn't have been anyone else.

"Yes. She asked me if you did this, and when I said no that you saved me, I just started crying. I couldn't stop. I told her what happened. Not the details, just enough."

"She seems like a nice person."

"She said that she'd like to have lunch or dinner with us sometime while we're here, but today I don't want to leave the room. I want to shower, sleep, eat here. Is that alright?"

"Of course. I drove all night. I could sleep until tomorrow."

"Can you order us some lunch first."

"I think so," Clint said.

They didn't leave the cabin that first day with Clint sleeping on the pull-out sofa sleeper and Frankie in the bed. The sleeping arrangements never changed, but he did get Frankie out of the cabin. Between long hikes and fishing out on the lake, Frankie started showing more signs of her old self.

On the third day there, Frankie called the police chief in Las Vegas and let him know she had been freed from her kidnappers and was going home to Hawaii. She said that hopefully in a month she would be able to return to Las Vegas, but she gave no promises. She also told him very bluntly that she didn't want to discuss what happened to her.

Five days after arriving at the lodge, they left and caught a plane in Seattle that took them to Honolulu. There they were met by Frankie's parents, and after a hug and a promise to stay on the island for a few days, Clint left her with her parents. He didn't hear from her for four days, so he sent her a text saying he was leaving. All he received back was an emoji of a heart.

Back in his car in Seattle, he rolled the gold coin around in his hand. His treasure, he thought. Buzz said it was a treasure, because they may never have discovered what the Chinese were up to without his setting into motion all that he had. Clint still considered it a curse; so many people had died or had been hurt.

Sitting alone, staring at nothing out his car window, he wondered where he should go next. After all, this was supposed to be a vacation. He rolled the coin between his fingers one last time, put it in his pocket, and drove away.

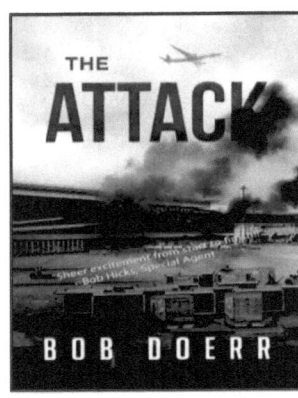

Title: *The Attack*™
Author: Bob Doerr
Publisher: TotalRecall Publications, Inc.
Paper Back: ISBN: 9781590951460
Book: ISBN: 9781590951477
Number of pages in the finished book:
Publication Date: 2014

A terrorist team has just set off four explosive devices in an international airport close to New York City. The leader of the terrorists, Ahmad Khalin, survives the attack and plans to attack a second U.S. airport within the month. As Khalin makes his escape from the New York area he is involved in a shooting in Connecticut. Clint Smith, a U.S. government agent assigned to an ultra-secret agency, is at a restaurant across the street when the shooting occurs. He responds to the scene to see if he can help, but Khalin is gone. On a hunch, Teresa Deer, Smith's boss, sends Smith after Khalin. Smith's pursuit takes him to Bar Harbor, Maine; Wiesbaden, Germany; the Costa Brava, Spain; Northern Scotland; Lake of the Woods, Ontario, Canada; and finally into Saskatchewan, Canada, where the final confrontation takes place. Throughout the pursuit, a number of interesting characters add to the subplots and try to survive their involvement in the chase.

A Clint Smith Thriller™

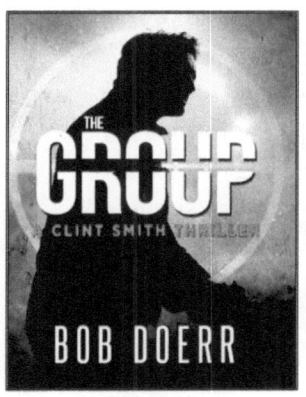

Title: *The Group*™
Author: Bob Doerr
Publisher: TotalRecall Publications, Inc.
Paper Back: ISBN: 9781590955697
eBook: ISBN: 9781590955703
Number of pages in the finished book: 288
Publication Date: 2016

A fast-moving international thriller that pits a lone government operative, known as a hunter, against an unknown group of assassins who pose a worldwide threat.

Someone is killing off the world's rich and famous. The murders are sophisticated, requiring precision and skill. The international community is in an uproar but has no leads in its attempt to find the assassins. The victims were members of the Bilderberg Group, an international, loose knit group of the uber rich that meet annually. While the attacks have not had a direct impact on the U.S., Theresa Deer, Director of the Special Section, a small unit whose existence is known by only a handful in the U.S. government, sees this new age League of Assassins as a national threat. She sends her hunters out. Clint Smith finds their trail Switzerland where his discovery almost leads to his own death. The hunt leads him to Mallorca, Spain, where he witnesses a helicopter attack on a villa where a number of attendees from the Bilderberg conference were holding a follow-on meeting of their own. Smith picks up the trail a couple weeks later in Las Vegas, NV, and in his hunt finds out that he is no longer the hunter. He has become the prey.

A Clint Smith Thriller™

Title: *The Assassins*™
Author: Bob Doerr
Publisher: TotalRecall Publications, Inc.
Paper Back: ISBN: 9781590951965
eBook: ISBN: 9781590951972
Number of pages in the finished book: 242
Publication Date: 2018

A disputed election has divided the nation, and a handful of senior government officials have conspired to have the North Koreans assassinate the President of the United States. Believing the assassination attempt to be only days away, Theresa Deer, Director of the Special Section, a small unit whose existence is known by only a few in the U.S. government, is tasked to interdict the man intent on providing the North Koreans vital information about the president's itinerary for his visit to South Korea. While Deer succeeds in her mission, she is severely injured and finds herself being hunted by the North Korean assassins. Clint Smith is sent to Korea to help Deer get back to the U.S. and finds himself caught in a deadly game of cat and mouse with the North Koreans. With no one in the U.S. government to turn to for help, and the South Koreans now also hunting them, getting out of South Korea alive is looking unlikely.

A Clint Smith Thriller™

Title: *The Treasure*™
Author: Bob Doerr
Publisher: TotalRecall Publications, Inc.
Paper Back: ISBN: 9781648830846
eBook: ISBN: 9781648830853
Number of pages in the finished book: 252
Publication Date: 2021

The Treasure is the fourth book in the Clint Smith thriller series. After a successful mission in South America, Clint heads to Las Vegas on vacation and to dig up a stagecoach strong box he had found in the desert earlier but had not opened. Upon inspection, he finds some old gold coins in mint condition and some well-preserved documents. He gives the contents of the strong box to a lawyer to find buyers. One of the documents, unfortunately, creates a maelstrom of violence and murder, and puts Clint squarely in the cross hairs of some Chinese assassins. Clint leaves Las Vegas to keep out of the spotlight, only to find himself going to Alaska in an attempt to rescue a female police officer who had been assigned to protect him in Las Vegas.

A Clint Smith Thriller™

Titles by Bob Doerr

Mystery Detective Suspense Thrillers

Dead Men Can Kill

Cold Winters Kill

Another Colorado Kill

Loose Ends Kill

No One Else To Kill

Caffeine Can Kill

Greed Can Kill

Honeymoons Can Kill'

Action Adventure Series

The Attack

The Group

The Assassins

The Treasure

Mouse Gate Series

The Enchanted Coin

The Rescue of Vincent

The Magic of Vex

Stranded in Space

Author Bob Doerr Uses his special knowledge to provide
authentic details in his novels about how
law enforcement agencies do their work.
For a complete list of books by Bob Doerr,
a preview of upcoming titles and more
visit his website.

www.bobdoerr.com

Locate Bob on Facebook and
let him know how you like his books.

www.ingramcontent.com/pod-product-compliance
Lightning Source LLC
Chambersburg PA
CBHW020619110726
47899CB00002B/573